## "A horse isn't that big a mystery. They show you what they need from you. Just like a man does."

Riley's voice had softened to a whisper. His gaze was intense, hypnotic. The need inside Dani swelled until she was dizzy.

He pulled her into his arms and lowered his face until their lips touched. In that moment every inkling of control vanished, melted in the heat of his kiss.

Dizzy with desire, Dani swayed against Riley. Her pulsing need vibrated through every erogenous cell in her body. She parted her lips and his tongue slipped inside her mouth. Thrusting. Probing. Ravenous. As if he couldn't get enough of her...

# QUICK-DRAW COWBOY

---

## JOANNA WAYNE

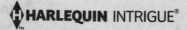

Thanks to all my friends and neighbors who've taught me so much about living in Texas. Now that I'm settled into my own small-town Texas lifestyle, I can't imagine living anywhere else. And, as always, thanks to my hubby for constantly being willing to rearrange our life to make time for my writing and research.

ISBN-13: 978-1-335-72096-2

Quick-Draw Cowboy

Copyright © 2017 by Jo Ann Vest

PLEASE RECYCLE
THIS PRODUCT IS RECYCLABLE

Recycling programs for this product may not exist in your area.

**Printed in U.S.A.**

HARLEQUIN®
™ www.Harlequin.com

**Joanna Wayne** began her professional writing career in 1994. Now, more than fifty published books later, Joanna has gained a worldwide following with her cutting-edge romantic suspense and Texas family series, such as Sons of Troy Ledger and Big "D" Dads. Joanna currently resides in a small community north of Houston, Texas, with her husband. You may write Joanna at PO Box 852, Montgomery, TX 77356, or connect with her at joannawayne.com.

## Books by Joanna Wayne

### Harlequin Intrigue

#### The Kavanaughs

*Riding Shotgun*
*Quick-Draw Cowboy*

#### Big "D" Dads: The Daltons

*Trumped Up Charges*
*Unrepentant Cowboy*
*Hard Ride to Dry Gulch*
*Midnight Rider*
*Showdown at Shadow Junction*
*Ambush at Dry Gulch*

#### Sons of Troy Ledger

*Cowboy Swagger*
*Genuine Cowboy*
*AK-Cowboy*
*Cowboy Fever*
*Cowboy Conspiracy*

#### Big "D" Dads

*Son of a Gun*
*Live Ammo*
*Big Shot*

Visit the Author Profile page at Harlequin.com for more titles.

# CAST OF CHARACTERS

*Dani Boatman*—Talented pastry chef and owner of Dani's Delights, a coffee shop and bakery in the charming and supposedly safe small town of Winding Creek, Texas.

*Riley Lawrence*—A hunky, rambling cowboy who loves his freedom and never stays in one place too long.

*Constance Boatman*—Dani's adorable and delightful orphaned niece who is the light of Dani's life, a child she would protect with her life.

*Grace Lawrence*—Dani's best friend since moving to Winding Creek.

*Pierce Lawrence*—Riley's brother, Grace's new husband and father of Jaci Lawrence.

*Tucker Lawrence*—Bull-rider brother to Pierce and Riley in town for Pierce and Grace's wedding.

*Amber Boatman*—Dani's late sister and Constance's mother.

*James Haggard*—A dangerous, demanding man who claims to be Constance's biological father.

*Lenny Haggard*—James's brother.

*Esther Kavanaugh*—The widow of Charlie Kavanaugh who loves the Lawrence brothers as if they were her own sons.

*Millie Miles*—Devoted mother to her troubled daughter, Angela.

*Angela Miles*—A flirty, sexy young woman who appears to have taken an odd route to handling her grief over her toddler son's death.

*Dudley Miles*—Had been Charlie Kavanaugh's best friend. Now in prison for manslaughter and trying to cover up the circumstances in the death of his beloved grandson.

# Chapter One

Dani Boatman piped the last exquisite rose onto the top layer of the tiered wedding cake. She stood back and examined her handiwork. Magnificent, she decided— *almost* too pretty to cut and eat.

But it would definitely be eaten. According to the bride, the guest list kept growing. Weddings were apparently a big deal in the small town of Winding Creek, Texas—a chance to dress up, visit with friends and neighbors and dance to a live band. And, of course, to celebrate the new couple.

The exciting part was that this time, she was not only invited to the festivities, but was also actually going to be involved. Maid of honor in the wedding of Grace Addison and Pierce Lawrence.

She'd be the only attendant, except for Pierce's five-year-old daughter, Jaci, who'd be the flower girl.

Grace had helped Dani pick out her dress, which was made of an emerald-green satin that brought out Dani's eyes and went well with her mass of unruly coppery curls.

The style worked, too. The dress was fitted at the waist with cap sleeves and a slightly flared skirt that fell to her ankles—easily long enough to cover her chunky calves.

The rounded, no-frills neckline revealed only a minimum of cleavage and fully covered her size 38 D puppies. A plump lady's version of chic.

Grace had been her first and only close friend since moving here. Not that the people weren't nice, but Dani's spare time amounted to pretty much zero.

Dani put the finishing touches on the cake, the last rose with petals so thin they were practically translucent. She'd entwined the roses with deep green vines to represent the way Grace and Pierce's lives had joined together forever.

Dani was a sucker for anything romantic. Not that she had any romance in her life. She'd dated, but never anything serious. Never met a guy who'd blown her away with just a smile, the way it happened in books.

Hadn't been with a guy who'd made her heart go tripping or left her breathless the way Grace claimed Pierce affected her.

But Dani was only twenty-six. One day her prince would come charging in on a white horse. Of course, with her luck, he'd probably be dropping by to order a wedding cake for his marriage to some hot chick with a drop-dead gorgeous body.

So, who needs a prince?

Dani had her very own bakery and she had her

adorable, drama-queen niece, Constance, who'd dropped into her life totally unexpectedly. Between her job and her niece, she was kept busy enough that she hit the bed exhausted every night.

And Dani was just about there now. She rubbed the tired muscles in her neck and glanced at the wall clock next to the cooling racks. Eighteen minutes after nine.

Not late by most people's standards for a Friday night, but she'd be up and baking before sunrise tomorrow morning. Fortunately all she had to do was descend the stairs from her second-floor living quarters and she was on the job.

She started cleaning the mess she'd made while icing the cake. The old building that housed her bakery was never totally quiet. It creaked and groaned at will, as if yesterday's ghosts still haunted the place that had originally been a bordello more than a century ago.

If only walls could talk.

Dani was startled from her mind's imaginative drifting at the sound of someone hammering a fist against the front door of the shop. The sign on the door clearly indicated they were closed and the lights in the serving section were out.

No one could be this desperate for a late-night sugar high.

She removed the chef's hat that kept her wild hair under control while she worked, and walked briskly to the front door of the shop. She arrived as the knocking started again. She flicked on the out-door light to see who was so rudely persistent.

The man who stared back at her looked harm-less enough. He was dressed in a pair of jeans and a blue plaid, long-sleeved sport shirt, open at the neck. Needed a haircut, but was clean-shaven. He looked a tad familiar, but she couldn't place him.

She motioned to the closed sign. The man didn't take the hint but kept standing there and waiting for her to let him in.

It was Friday night, so there were still a few peo-ple out and about in Winding Creek's downtown area. A couple were leaving the pharmacy across the street. A family of four with ice-cream cones were checking out the display window of a candle shop next to the pharmacy. A group of twentysomethings spilled out of a double cab pickup truck and into the middle of Main Street, no doubt headed to Caffe's Bar and Grill around the corner.

The man at her door looked no more of a threat than the rest of them. Besides which, the town of Winding Creek was practically crime-free. She pulled the key ring from her pocket, unlocked the door and opened it a crack.

"We're closed," she said. "Open again at seven tomorrow morning."

"Sorry to bother you, but I think I left my wind-breaker here earlier today."

The pieces suddenly fell together. He was obviously the man who'd left the jacket she'd found on the floor beneath one of the tables.

"Was it blue?"

"Yep. Navy blue."

"I'll get it for you."

He put a foot in the door, basically inviting himself inside. His pushiness irritated her and made her a bit nervous.

She checked to make sure her cell phone was still attached to the waistband of her flour-splattered slacks. A call to 911 would have a deputy at her door in seconds. There would always be at least one in the downtown area on Friday evenings.

"Nice place you have here," he said. "Dani's Delights, catchy name, too."

"Thank you. I'll be right back with your jacket."

She retreated to her office off the kitchen, picked up the jacket and took her cell phone in her right hand. When she turned around, the man was standing a few feet from her, blocking the door.

"Here's your jacket," she said. "You can go now."

"After we talk."

His attitude alarmed her. "We have nothing to talk about."

"Yes, we do." He took a step toward her, almost backing her against her desk.

Every muscle tensed. "If it's conversation you want, I'll yell and my husband will rush down the stairs to join the chat. I should warn you, he's an excellent shot and will be toting a forty-five."

"You don't have a husband, but you do have *my* daughter. So now that we have the essentials out of the way, why don't we sit down and discuss this quietly like two rational adults?"

"I don't know who you think you're talking to, but you've obviously mistaken me for someone else."

"No. I know exactly who you are, and that you were granted custody of my daughter, Constance Boatman. That's where the mistakes comes in. I'm her father, which makes me next of kin—not you."

"You're lying." The words had flown to her mouth. Only she couldn't be sure of their accuracy. She had no idea who Constance's father was. She had her niece's birth certificate filed away in her upstairs living quarters, where Constance was sleeping right now. No father was listed. She was certain of that.

The social workers who'd testified in the custody hearing had insisted there was no record of the father's identity. That had been eight months ago, weeks after her sister, Amber's, tragic death. If he was the father, where had he been all this time?

"Who are you?" she demanded.

"You know my name. James Haggard. It's on the birth certificate. Your sister, Amber, and I were very much in love back then. Your niece is a love child, if that matters to you. That was before your sister let the addiction turn her into a slut."

"My sister is dead and I will not tolerate you talking about her that way. Get out now or I will call the police."

"Not a good idea. Once the law gets involved, things get really sticky. I prove I'm Constance's birth father, I get custody. Case closed. Trust me, I'd make a lousy father. She's better off with you."

That she believed, but she refused to accept he had any claim on Constance. But what if he did? Someone contributed the sperm that led to her birth. That person might well be an obnoxious jerk like James Haggard.

From the time Amber turned sixteen and moved out, she had slept with any man who'd supply her with drugs. And her sister had ignored both their mother's tears and Dani's constant pleading for Amber to go into rehab. Their mother had never fully recovered from the heartbreak.

Dani's precious niece was all she had left of the sister who had meant the world to her. She wouldn't turn her over to this irresponsible jerk even if he was her biological father.

Dani's stomach retched. She had to deal with this. "What is it you want?"

"My share of the insurance settlement from the car manufacturer. The faulty air bag that led to my dear, sweet daughter losing her mother earned you a hefty payout."

"I should have known it was greed that brought you here."

"Don't be so pious, Dani. This little business setup you have here didn't come cheap. You didn't pay for it with pocket change."

"No, which is why I'm up to my eyeballs in debt." Not that it was any of his business.

"Don't try to pull one on over me. I've had all of that I'm putting up with. I know how much the pay-off was. By my estimates, even after you paid for the bakery and the lawyers took their share, I figure you have at least a couple of million dollars left. I deserve all of that, but to show you what a nice man I am, I'll settle for a mere million. In cash. In one week."

"You…" Dani bit back the words she wanted to hurl at him. They wouldn't phase a lowlife like him. Yet she could easily believe he would have gotten Amber pregnant and then abandoned her and the baby.

Amber had been a stunning beauty before her addiction took its toll, just as James Haggard said. She'd had long auburn hair that fell in loose curls about her shoulders, gorgeous amber-colored eyes, lush eyelashes and a dynamite body.

Amber had always been the pretty sister. Everyone had said it. The comments had cut Dani to the quick when they were growing up. That hadn't changed the fact that she worshipped her older sister.

Now it was Constance who mattered more than anything.

"Even if you are Constance's father—which I seriously doubt—you're wrong about the insurance money. It's all in a trust fund for Constance and can't be touched until she turns twenty-one."

"Yet you found a way to get your greedy little

hands on it," the man snarled. "And you can cut the pretense. We both know you have at least a copy of the birth certificate that lists me as the father."

She shook her head. She'd had enough. "You're wrong. Now get out. And stay away from here. If you show up again, I'll call the sheriff and press harassment charges."

He glared at her, his eyes dark and penetrating, and it was almost as if she could feel a bizarre mix of evil and madness fighting for his soul.

Chills ran up her spine, but she stood her ground. She pointed to the door. "Out. Now."

"I'm leaving, but I'll be back next week for the stacks. If you don't have all the big ones, I'll not only file for paternal custody, but have you prosecuted for stealing my daughter's money. Is that what you want?"

"You won't have a prayer of getting custody without proof of paternity. Bluffing won't help you. DNA won't lie for you."

"DNA won't have to lie. In the meantime, take care of my beloved daughter." He smiled at his own sarcastic quip, turned and walked away.

Anger and dread left Dani shaking. This was blackmail, plain and simple. A scam. A bluff. James Haggard's name was not on the birth certificate.

But what if a paternity test proved he was Constance's father? Was there a judge alive who'd actually take a child who'd been through what Constance had suffered and rip her from this safe, secure life, where she was loved?

Would any judge grant custody to a man who'd abandoned his child and her addicted mother years before? Wouldn't a judge realize that Haggard was in this strictly to find a way to get at Constance's trust fund?

But then, crazier things happened in the court system every day.

"I've told you the insurance is in an untouchable trust and there's no way I can come up with the amount of money you're talking about."

"Then I guess I'll just have to do that myself—once I have custody of Constance." He started to the door, then turned and pointed at her as if he was pulling a trigger. "Next Friday. Before noon."

She waited until she heard the front door slam behind Haggard before she walked over and locked the door behind him.

She looked out the huge front window and stared at the dance of light and shadows beneath the antique streetlights. Winding Creek was the ideal, small Texas town. Friendly. Safe.

A place where Constance could heal from the ordeals she'd endured living with Amber and her addictions. A home where she felt protected and loved after years of neglect and frequent abandonment by her own mother. That had been the deciding factor in Dani's going into debt to open her own bakery here.

James Haggard had shattered that illusion.

Dani went back to the kitchen to finish cleaning up. The cake she'd worked hours on meant nothing to her as Haggard's vicious threats echoed through her mind.

She was not convinced he was Constance's father, but she was certain he'd told the truth about at least one thing.

He would be back.

## Chapter Two

Ten o'clock on Saturday in downtown Winding Creek, Texas. Not just any Saturday. This was the date Riley Lawrence's older brother, Pierce, was giving marriage a second chance. Sounded downright crazy to Riley. He'd never had the guts to tie the knot even once and didn't plan to remedy that any time soon.

Riley figured it was too early for a beer even though he'd been driving since five that morning after a few hours of restless sleep. The motel bed had left a lot to be desired in the way of comfort.

Not that comfort mattered all that much to him. He'd slept under the stars many a night with no more than a rolled-up jacket for a pillow.

He turned onto Main Street. He'd expected at least a fleeting sensation that he was home again. Didn't happen. The town looked almost exactly the same as when he'd lived here until just before his fifteenth birthday. It also looked completely different.

Perspective changed everything.

When he'd lived here, Winding Creek was all he

really knew. Now he'd seen most of the country, at least the parts of it he was interested in seeing. Any place he hung his Stetson was home.

He should probably just keep driving and head straight to the Double K Ranch, but as eager as he was to see his brothers, he wasn't quite ready to dive into wedding chaos. He definitely wasn't eager to start hiding his doubts about Pierce's decision to jump into the fire again.

He pulled his old black pickup truck into a parking spot, got out and stretched. The antique streetlights were familiar. So were the buildings. Even a few old hitching posts were still scattered along the curb.

The storefronts were a different story. The old Texaco station was now a sandwich shop. The barbershop where he'd gotten his hair cut as a kid was now a candle shop. Who'd have guessed you needed a separate shop to buy candles?

He glanced at the signs. An ice-cream parlor. A Christmas store. A toy shop. Even a jewelry store. Practically a shopping mecca compared to where he'd been living in Montana.

He caught a whiff of coffee and followed the scent to a bakery. Dani's Delights. The cookies, scones and cupcakes displayed in the window looked incredible, but it was the aroma of the day's grind that lured him in.

The dozen or so tables in the place were all taken. The line to order was at least ten people deep. He wasn't sure any cup of coffee was worth that kind of wait.

Easy to see the problem. There was only one person to take orders, collect money and mix the fancy coffee drinks. The woman behind the counter looked a bit harried and her smile was clearly forced.

He continued to study her as he stepped into the line. A full head shorter than his six foot two. Heart-shaped face. Cute upturned nose. A mass of wild cinnamon-colored curls that hugged her cheeks.

Maybe her coffee was worth waiting in line for after all. Marriage and commitment might scare him half to death, but that didn't mean he couldn't enjoy the company of a vivacious woman every now and then.

Women were in short supply on the ranch where he'd been living in Montana. Available women were nonexistent.

Riley inched up when the line moved and glanced around the small shop. He recognized Dan Dupree, who was sitting in the back with who were probably his grandkids. Dan and his wife had been friends of Riley's parents before their fatal car accident.

Mrs. Maclean, Riley's ninth-grade English teacher, was at another table with two women he didn't recognize. Neither Dan nor Mrs. Maclean showed any sign of recognizing him.

Fortunately, he'd changed from the skinny, awkward, pimpled teenager he'd been last time he lived in Winding Creek. He'd added a few inches in height and muscled up a bit.

The door opened and four more people squeezed in and joined the line.

A freckle-faced kid with braided red hair, eyeglasses and cut-off jeans ran noisily down some back stairs that led into the bakery. She maneuvered around the sign at the foot of the stairs that read Private. Do Not Enter. Prancing like a showy filly, she made her way across the shop.

The youngster propped her elbows on the far end of the counter. "I'm bored," she announced loud enough for everyone in the shop to hear.

"Did you finish your homework?" the busy woman asked without looking up from the display case, where she was gathering raspberry scones for her customer.

"Yes, except for the math. I hate word problems. They don't even make sense."

"They make sense, Constance, but I'll help you with your homework later. I'm really busy right now. Why don't you watch TV upstairs until Sally and her mother pick you up for the movie?"

"I'm tired of being upstairs by myself. I wanna stay down here, Aunt Dani."

Ah, aunt. Not the kid's mother. Made sense. She didn't look old enough for that. He checked out the busy redhead's ring finger. No golden band. Looking better all the time.

"Can I have a cookie?" the girl asked.

"Not before lunch. You know the rules," the aunt answered as she added whipped cream to a coffee drink.

The kid's hands flew to her hips. "Everybody else in here has a cookie, or a muffin, or something."

"We'll talk about this later, Constance."

Constance rolled her eyes. Quite a performer and with an attitude. Call him crazy, but Riley liked that about her.

The woman in line behind Riley began to complain. "I just came in here to pick up a birthday cake I ordered a week ago for my daughter. At this rate, the party will be over before I get the cake."

"Guess there's a run on coffee and scones this morning," Riley said. "But the woman's working as fast as she can."

"Dani needs to hire more help for her shop on Saturdays. Then she wouldn't have to do everything herself."

So the woman behind the counter was also the owner of Dani's Delights. Interesting.

The next person to approach the counter gave a to-go order for four cups of plain coffee, two-flavored lattes and a mixture of pastries.

Dani was still smiling, but she had to be overwhelmed. At least the little girl was helping now, keeping the customers in line entertained with a series of funny faces.

Riley stepped out of line and walked up to the counter. "You look like you could use some help."

"You think? I had two teenage workers not show up this morning without bothering to call in and let me know."

"Big night in town last night?"

"Not that I know of. Anyway, sorry for the delay, but I'm moving as fast as I can."

"I wasn't complaining. In fact, I have a proposition that's too good to refuse."

"I don't know," she said, without looking up. "I'm extremely good at saying no."

She bagged the pastries for the current order and started on the lattes. "What's your offer?"

"Behind-the-counter help. I can handle pouring coffee, but I could never concoct those fancy drinks you're making. By the way, my name's Riley Lawrence."

Dani looked up, a slightly surprised expression parting her full lips. "You must be Pierce's brother."

"Yep, but don't hold that against me."

"Never. Pierce is terrific and marrying my best friend. I'm sure he's thrilled you made it here for the wedding," she said as she went back to boxing pastries. "He was afraid you'd back out at the last minute."

"I was a bit afraid of that myself. Actually, I haven't made it to the Double K yet."

"Then what in the world are you doing here?"

"Saving your beautiful ass—pardon my French. That is if you want my help."

"You're serious?"

"Serious as a bull on steroids."

"I have no idea what that means, but you've got yourself a job."

"How about we start two lines?" Riley suggested. "One for the people who want specialty coffees and-or want to pay with credit cards. Another line of the people who just want plain coffee or to pick up some bakery items and pay with cash."

"You'll handle the cash line?"

"Yep. I've had very limited experience with cash registers, but that one doesn't look too complicated."

She sighed. "It would be a tremendous help, but I can't let you do that."

"Afraid I'll sneak too many cookies?"

"No. Afraid Esther will kill me for delaying your arrival at the ranch."

The door opened again. This time a family of four came in, stretching the line around the corner.

"If the line grows any longer, you may have a mutiny on your hands."

"Okay, but remember you asked for this. Prices are marked on the items on display," Dani explained. "Preordered items are boxed and in the kitchen right behind us. Name of the customer and price are on the ticket taped to the top of the box. If you have any questions, just ask."

Dani raised her voice to get everyone's attention and explained the new lineup procedures. Someone clapped and several more joined in. They moved into the two lines with amazing order and good manners.

That was the Winding Creek he remembered.

"By the way, my name's Dani Boatman," she offered.

"Glad to meet you, boss."

His first customer spoke up. "I'm picking up a dozen cupcakes for Jamie Sandler. She ordered them yesterday."

"Coming right up."

And with that Riley was officially on the job. He'd never sold anything in his life, except horses or cattle at an auction and admission tickets once at a local rodeo in Wyoming. His cash-register experience was limited to gate ticket sales.

Turned out this was much easier. Almost everybody was friendly and happier now that the line was moving a little faster.

The guys gave him a howdy, several introducing themselves. It was the Texas way. Young women—and some of the older ones—flirted with him. A little boost for the ego.

None of the females were as tempting as Dani Boatman. He might just be staying around Winding Creek a little longer than originally planned.

Two HOURS LATER, the Saturday morning rush had come and gone. Only three tables were occupied and there was no one in line. Constance was off to the movie with her friend.

And Dani Boatman was totally infatuated with the witty, personable, hunky cowboy who'd saved the day. But then he'd charmed almost every woman who'd walked into the bakery. Some men had a knack for winning hearts with just a smile. Riley had it in spades.

"Whew..." Riley said. "Are Saturday mornings always this busy?"

"Unfortunately, no. They're my busiest day of the week, but not usually this kind of crazy. The sunny day and the wildflowers in full bloom brought out the tourists."

"I get that. I'm not much of a flower man, but even I noticed the sea of bluebonnets driving in this morning. Damned impressive."

"You'd be amazed how many people visit the Texas Hill Country every spring just for the scenery."

"Scenery in here looks pretty good to me."

"Thanks. I try to make the pastries too tempting to resist."

He smiled seductively. "I wasn't talking about the pastries."

A flush of heat crept up her face. She turned away quickly, hoping he hadn't noticed the blush. He'd think she was either incredibly naive, or had never had a man casually flirt with her.

Tough to admit, but neither was that far-fetched.

"Did you bake all this?" he asked, motioning to the display cases full of her cookies, cupcakes, scones and other pastries, as well as loaves of bread.

"Yes."

"And you babysit your niece. When do you have time for a life?"

"This is my life. And I don't babysit Constance. My sister died this past year. Constance lives with me."

"So it's just you and Constance?"

"That's it."

"Instant motherhood. That must have thrown your life into a tailspin."

"It's been an adjustment, but I'm loving it. We live above the shop so I can be with her as much as possible."

The door opened again and Sandy O'Malley rushed in, her short skirt swinging around her thighs, her long blond hair pulled back in a ponytail. "I'm so sorry, Miss Boatman. My alarm didn't go off this morning. I mean I know I set it, but it didn't go off and Mom had gone into work early and I guess I got to bed late and…"

"Take a breath, Sandy," Dani said, stopping the onslaught of excuses. "We'll talk later. For now, you can start clearing the tables."

"Yes, ma'am. I'll get right to it."

"Guess I'm officially replaced," Riley said.

"Yes, but you saved me from total chaos this morning. If there's anything I can do to thank you for jumping into the madness…"

"Let me give it some thought. I'm sure we can think of a way. Will I see you at the wedding tonight?"

"Can't miss me. I'm the maid of honor."

"How 'bout that? I'm one of the two best men. Pierce had to give his brothers equal billing. I've yet to meet the bride, but according to Pierce, she hung the moon and outshines most of the stars."

"And she's just as crazy about him. They're a perfect couple."

"More than a couple," Riley said. "They have Pierce's five-year-old daughter, Jaci, at least part-time. They'll be an instant family with all the complications that can bring. Glad it's him and not me."

Which was in perfect agreement with how Pierce had described his brother. Riley was a rambler, never stayed in one place long enough to get serious about any woman. The love-'em-and-leave-'em type.

"I'll see you tonight," Riley said. "Save me a two-stepper. I hear there's going to be a country-and-western band."

"Sure." As if he'd notice a short, plump pastry chef once he was besieged by every other woman there.

"Thanks again for helping out," she said. "If you ever need a steady job with long hours, low pay and lots of work, give me a call."

"I appreciate that generous offer, but unfortunately I start to rust if I spend more than a couple of hours indoors. See you tonight."

She watched Riley walk away. That was when she saw James Haggard staring at her through the window. She braced herself to deal with him, but he made no move to enter the shop. He just continued to stare, every muscle in his face stretched taut.

There was no doubt that he meant to intimidate her, to make her shudder in fear and realize that he'd meant what he said.

She'd lain awake for hours last night, considering his threats, trying to decide what her next move should be. She'd told the truth about the money being in a trust fund—it had been at Dani's insistence. That didn't mean that as Constance's father, Haggard couldn't challenge her decision.

If he was her biological father.

All she needed was a sample of his DNA to prove him wrong. Or prove him right.

If she could somehow get a sample of his DNA, she could have the testing done without his cooperation. But then why wouldn't he cooperate? He didn't want Constance. He wanted to basically sell her for a million dollars.

If he wasn't her biological father, Dani would report him and his rotten scam to the sheriff. If he was… She couldn't bring herself to go there now.

She was closing at three today, an hour earlier that her usual time to make the sundown wedding without too much of a rush. She'd search paternity testing labs in San Antonio before she left for the Double K Ranch, to get the facts about how to go about the testing.

And then she'd insist Haggard provide a DNA

sample. If he refused, that was as good as an admission that he was lying.

No matter what the results, she had to keep Constance out of the hands of James Haggard. If it came down to it, she'd protect her niece from scum like him with her life.

# Chapter Three

Riley propped a booted foot on a bag of feed. It was the first time he'd managed a few minutes alone with Pierce and their younger brother, Tucker. They'd taken a walk out to the barn to get some privacy.

"So you're serious about staying on here at the Double K?" Riley asked. "As a hired hand?"

"Not exactly. Esther and I have been talking. She's willing to sell me the ranch as long as she can keep her house, her gardens and her chickens. I'd never dream of taking those from her anyway. As you know, Grace, Jaci and me are living with her now and it's working out fine."

"I just never figured she'd sell the Double K."

"Frankly, she doesn't have the resources to keep it going, and to be honest, I've never been as happy as I've been these past few months. I have some money saved and this seems like the perfect investment."

"Last time we were together, you said you'd never been happier than being a Navy SEAL," Riley said.

"That was the truth then and exactly what I needed at that time in my life. But this life is the kind of satisfaction that seeps bone-deep. Not just the ranch, though I sure feel I belong here, but it's Grace and Jaci and, I don't know, man. It just feels so right."

"Don't you just have temporary custody of your daughter until her mother and new stepfather get back to the States?" Tucker asked.

"Yes, but we're working on more permanent arrangements. It seems Leslie's new husband will be working on the project in Cuba longer than expected. We're talking about joint custody, but with Jaci spending summers and most holidays with her mother and the rest of the time with me and Grace."

"How does Jaci feel about that?"

"She loves the ranch. Well, mostly she loves horses, but she's handling the divorce like a trouper. We're family. She even calls Esther 'Grandmother' and Grace 'Mommy.'"

"And Esther seems to love that," Tucker said.

"So getting married so soon after meeting Grace doesn't frighten you at all?" Riley asked.

"Not in the least."

"You've definitely been roped and tied," Tucker said.

"Except I was the one doing the roping. I was hooked from practically the moment I met Grace. When I thought I was going to lose her to a madman, I knew for certain my life would never be complete without her."

"I guess that explains the rush to the altar," Riley said.

"I was ready to marry her the day after she said yes. She was the one who encouraged me to wait until you two could actually coordinate your schedules enough to show up for the ceremony. She's big on family ties."

"It all sounds great," Riley agreed, "but you were madly in love before and look how that worked out."

"I failed in that marriage," Pierce admitted. "Leslie and I were like two horses pulling in different directions. There was no way we were going to arrive at the same destination."

"But you got Jaci out of that marriage," Tucker said. "She's a terrific kid, so it wasn't a total loss."

"Exactly," Pierce confirmed.

And Riley should probably leave it at that, but what kind of brother would he be if he didn't say what he was thinking?

"You haven't known Grace very long. What happens if you and Grace start pulling in opposite directions? Another divorce? More emotional trauma for Jaci?"

"I get your concerns," Pierce said. "But I have no doubts about Grace or my love for her. It's about love, but it's also about shared experiences and trust and knowing that the other person will always be there for you. Grace and I have that."

"Then I guess you're ready for the marriage game."

"It's not a game," Pierce argued.

"Right. It's your life. If you're happy, then I couldn't be happier for you."

Riley meant that. It was just that settling down to one woman, one ranch, one set of options seemed a lot like sticking a horse in one pasture and never letting it taste the grass on the other side of the fence.

"To change the subject, do you guys remember our first day on the Double K Ranch?" Tucker asked.

"All too well," Pierce said. "I was scared to open my mouth, afraid Esther and Charlie would kick us out if we did anything to annoy them."

"Same here," Riley said. "And if we got rejected by the Kavanaughs, that scary old hag of a social worker would take over and place us in three different foster homes."

"I cried the day the social worker said that," Tucker said, "but I hid so you two couldn't see me. At twelve, I figured I was way too old to cry."

The truth was they'd all had trouble dealing with the grief. One morning they'd had loving parents, a home, security. A few hours later a policeman showed up at the door and told them their parents had died in a car crash.

They'd spent the next ten months with Charlie and Esther before a great-uncle they'd never met showed up and took them to live in Kansas with him until they turned eighteen.

But Riley had never truly gotten over that feeling that he was one second away from a catastrophe. Maybe none of them had. Could be that was why Tucker risked his life almost daily riding two-thousand-pound bulls that would just as soon crack his skull with a hoof as not.

Maybe that was why Pierce had become a Navy SEAL and had been so good at it. And the reason Riley could never commit to anything. There was no certainty of anything in life.

Or maybe they were all just three brothers out there trying to find where they fit.

"I had a few minutes alone with Esther this morning," Tucker said. "She still seems to think Charlie was murdered."

"I know," Pierce said. "I've looked in to it some, but there's just no evidence to support that."

"Yet hard to believe he committed suicide," Riley said. "Were there health issues?"

"Not that Esther's mentioned," Pierce said. "But like I said, there are lots of money issues. The ranch is mortgaged to the hilt and Charlie was behind in his payments. His bank account is down to a few thousand dollars and he'd been steadily selling off his livestock since the drought two years ago."

Riley leaned against a bale of hay. "Looks like your offer to buy in came just in time to save the ranch."

"It's working out that way," Pierce agreed. "It's great for Esther, too. She gets to stay in her home she shared with Charlie for so many years and still tend to her beloved chickens and her vegetable garden. Charlie's ranch doesn't fall into the hands of the bank. It's a win-win all the way around."

"Except that you're buying a ranch that you admit has fallen into a state of serious disrepair."

"I like a challenge. Besides, I had some money saved, thinking I might buy a ranch. Even after I pay off the debts, I'll have enough left to hopefully make the Double K a profitable operation again."

"You've got your work cut out for you," Riley said.

"Yep, and I'm hoping my brother the rambler might settle down for a few months and help me out."

"Why did I not see this coming?" Strangely, Riley wasn't put off by the idea. He had to be somewhere; might as well be here helping out his brother and Esther—for a while.

"Just don't get any ideas that I'm going to settle down in Winding Creek forever, big brother."

"That possibility never entered my mind."

So now the cute, little redheaded pastry chef with the sparkling eyes and the heart-melting smile wasn't his only excuse for hanging around Winding Creek.

"You think we have time to saddle a few horses and race out to the swimming hole like old times?" Tucker asked.

"I don't see why not," Pierce said. "I'm banned from seeing my bride until the wedding and it's not going to take me long to shower and struggle into the monkey suit."

"Now you're talking," Riley said.

The three Lawrence brothers racing on horseback once again. This was as good as it got.

## Chapter Four

Riley stood with Pierce and Tucker a couple of yards to the left of the flowered arbor, where the minister was patiently waiting.

Guests had been arriving for the past half hour or more, filling up the rows of folding chairs.

Riley recognized very few of them. "You must be giving away a new tractor to draw this many people."

"And to think this started out as a small family wedding," Pierce said."

"You've only been back here on a permanent basis since Christmas. Do you even know half these people?" Tucker asked.

"Not many, but Esther knows them all. Once she got involved in the plans, the size of the wedding at least quadrupled. We didn't have the heart to reel her in. The busier she is, the better she does with handling the grief over Charlie's death."

"This must have cost a fortune," Riley said. "Did you win the lottery and forget to tell me?"

"Nope. But this is Texas. You have a shindig,

everyone chips in to help. The only food we had to furnish were the briskets that I smoked myself. And the booze, of course, though not even all of that. Some old friend of Charlie's I've never even seen before dropped off a few cases of beer today."

"They've been bringing in food for a good hour," Tucker said. "I guess we'll find out who the best cooks in the area are."

"None better than Esther," Pierce assured them, "though I doubt you'll find a bad dish in the bunch."

"Then I guess I'll have to try them all," Tucker said. "You lucked out with the weather, but what were you going to do if it rained? If I remember correctly, this area turns into a giant mud puddle with every shower."

"We had the option of moving the affair to the new community center next to the high school. The folding chairs and tables belong to the center anyway. The portable dance floor, too, though I had to rent it. Cost me a whopping twenty-five dollars."

"And all the lights you've got strung through branches and around poles?"

"Those I bought and Esther's part-time wrangler, Buck, and some of his buddies set them up."

"I didn't buy a wedding present," Tucker said. "Figured if there was something you needed, you already had it. Why don't I throw in some money to cover the cost of the reception tent?"

"Appreciated, but not necessary. One of Charlie's

good friends, Harvey Mullins, has a son in San Antonio who rents party supplies."

Harvey had insisted on providing the tent with no
charge for it, or for putting it up and taking it down.
He said Charlie had helped him rebuild his barn last
year when lightning had hit and he was glad to do
something to repay the favor.

"Sounds like this is a community affair, so who
do I see about filing a formal complaint?" Riley
quipped.

"File thirteen is behind the woodshed. What are
you complaining about?"

"This straitjacket I'm buttoned into. Shirt's so stiff
I can barely move."

"I couldn't get Grace to budge on that, but she
did agree to our wearing our cowboy boots as long
as we had then cleaned and shined."

"What a woman," Riley said. "All heart."

"The real question is, does she have a friend for
Riley?" Tucker said.

Thankfully they didn't get to finish the conversation. The music started and they were motioned into
place by the minister.

Riley watched as someone he didn't recognize
escorted Esther to her seat. He wasn't sure if Esther
was acting as mother of the bride or mother of the
groom, but she was smiling and dabbing at her eyes
at the same time.

He knew what having the Kavanaughs take them
in for ten months after their parents died meant to

him and his brothers. He guessed he never fully realized what it had meant to Esther and, no doubt, to Charlie. From now on, he'd see that he kept in closer touch.

He flashed Esther a smile and looked over to see if Pierce was starting to panic yet. Nope. The man had ice water in his veins. Must be all that SEAL training.

When Riley looked up again, Dani was walking down the makeshift aisle between the rows of folding chairs. The wow factor sent his head spinning. She'd been cute and witty in the bakery. She was absolutely stunning in a brilliant green dress that set off her gorgeous eyes.

Damn, he even liked the way she walked. She didn't glide or prance like some haughty mare. She just walked, like a gal who knew who she was and what she was about.

Would be right interesting to check her out a little further, find out if she was as authentic as she seemed. If he hung around awhile, they could have some good times before he hit the road again.

Horseback riding up to the gorge at Lonesome Branch. Do some fishing for bream or catfish. Maybe even take a dip in the swimming hole if the weather cooperated.

Desire revved inside him at the thought of her in—or out of—a bikini.

When she reached the arbor, her gaze met his. She smiled and suddenly all he could think about was getting the wedding over with and getting his arms around her on the dance floor.

The rest of the wedding procession barely registered with him until it was time for him to hand Pierce the ring. He watched as Pierce slid it onto Grace's finger. He saw the way they looked at each other and he had to admit it did look like love.

But then this was the easy part of a marriage—when everything about the relationship was new and exciting. Before the ties didn't bind. Before hard times and resentments started pulling a couple apart.

Riley didn't see himself ever vowing to love anyone or anything for forever. Yet, when the happy couple were pronounced man and wife and Pierce kissed his bride, Riley hoped with all his heart that marriage worked this time for Pierce and Grace. And mostly for his five-year-old niece, Jaci.

Riley had dreaded coming to this wedding, but now that it was nearly over, he had to admit he'd never seen his brother happier. Even more of a shocker, Riley was looking forward to the rest of the evening. He was downright excited about getting to know Dani better.

For all the roving around from ranch to ranch and from state to state that he did, could it be that he was the one in a rut?

No. He was a born wanderer and he liked it that way.

But if he was ready to settle down, he'd be looking for a woman who had it all together. He'd be looking for a woman like Dani.

"THAT'S GOOD. LET'S get one more shot before we lose that sunset. Just the women this time. Esther, Grace, Dani and our little flower girl."

Not the words Dani had hoped to hear. The air was cooling off as the sun made its final descent, but the Texas humidity had not let up. She could feel herself starting to wilt like a rosebush in a heat wave.

The wedding had been beautiful and touching and perfect in every way, but the photographer was getting a bit carried away with his after-ceremony wedding-party shots. Dani was not the only one growing restless. Jaci kept sneaking away from the group only to be tugged back by one of the adults.

"If we move a few yards to the left, we can—"

"Whoa there," Pierce interrupted. "Feels like Miller time to me. I'm sure that's enough pictures of this group."

"Are you sure?" Tucker queried. "I thought we were going for Prince William and Kate's record."

"Okay, okay," the photographer said, relenting. "Just trying to give you your money's worth."

Jaci tugged on Pierce's hand. "Can I go play now, Daddy?"

"I think we're all ready to go and play," Grace said. "But before you all scatter, I want to say thank you one more time for being part of our wedding. You've made the happiest day of my life even more special by sharing it with us."

Pierce put an arm around her. "That goes for me,

too. And, bros, I'll be sure and be there when you tie the knot."

"Find me a winner like Grace and I'm in," Tucker said.

DANI REACHED FOR a glass of bubbly from the tray of full flutes someone had been nice enough to bring them. Scanning the area, she quickly spotted Constance with her good friend Sally and a couple of other school friends. They were ceremoniously sliding across the portable dance floor in their socks while the band set up their instruments.

Happy. Surrounded by friends. Watched over by Sally's mother, Crystal. Safe.

But for how long? Dani shuddered. She'd done a good job of keeping James Haggard out of her mind during the ceremony, but now he was back and tormenting her thoughts.

She'd found several labs in San Antonio that promised quick results with paternity testing.

She ordered a DNA collection kit online from Corinthian Court Labs and paid extra for overnight delivery. With luck, she'd have it in her hands by Monday morning.

The next time Haggard dropped by, she'd insist he cooperate. She seriously doubted she'd have to wait until Friday to see him again.

Having a plan helped but didn't alleviate her apprehension.

"Are you okay, dear? You look like you've checked out of this hoopla."

Esther's words of concern jolted Dani back to the present. "I'm fine, but I'd best get back to the reception area and help control Constance."

"I'll walk with you. Jaci, why don't you come with us and we'll check out the party?"

Jaci clapped her hands and skipped over to join them.

As the photographer folded his tripod, several guests rushed up to congratulate the groom and hug the beaming bride. Riley and Tucker were quickly accosted, as well, by two very attractive young women. Dani had seen both of them in the bakery a few times, but didn't actually know them. In their early twenties, she'd guess. Both thin as a blade of grass.

Not that Dani cared. She'd never expected any more from Riley than a dance and she wasn't putting much faith in that. He certainly didn't owe her anything.

Dani picked up her pace, determined not to be annoyed by the sound of Riley's laughter, probably at something one of the flaunting flirts had whispered in his ear.

By the time she reached Constance, the little manipulator and Sally were swiping maraschino cherries from a tray on the portable bar in back of the tent.

"That's enough," Crystal said. "You'll get a stomach-ache and no one else will get any cherries in their drinks."

Dani tiptoed up and surprised Constance with a quick hug. "How about a glass of orange juice instead?"

"Or a couple of Shirley Temples," the cute young cowboy behind the bar suggested.

Constance's mouth flew open and she covered it with her hand, her eyes wide as she looked up at Dani and then back to the bartender. "My aunt would kill me if I drank that."

Dani laughed. "You can have a Shirley Temple if you like."

"I can?"

"Sure. It's not alcohol."

"What is it?"

"It's sort of like a Sprite with a cherry."

"Oh. Then I'll just have a Sprite with a cherry in it."

"Me, too," Sally said.

Crystal stepped around the girls. "And I'll have a white wine."

"Coming right up." The bartender took his time with them with little concern for a couple of guys waiting on service.

"My feet are killing me," Crystal said, reaching down to make an adjustment on the strap. "And these shoes felt so good when I tried them on in the shop."

"Have you guys eaten yet?" Dani asked.

"We have," Crystal said. "Food is great, especially

the brisket sliders and Esther's fabulous creamed-corn casserole, but I controlled myself. Have to save room for wedding cake."

"Your cake is beautiful," Sally said. "When I get married, I want you to bake my cake and make it as tall as me."

"Why don't I just practice on a few birthday cakes shorter than you first?" Dani responded.

"I second that," Crystal said. "We're a long way from talking weddings."

The bartender handed them their drinks.

"I'll carry your drink," Crystal said, reaching for Dani's flute of champagne. "You can grab a plate of food while the girls and I snag seats—away from the band, so we can talk about how beautiful the wedding was and how smashing you look."

"Thanks. I like smashing." She had felt rather smashing until she'd compared herself to the two model-thin ladies hitting on Riley and Tucker. That had put things back into perspective pretty quickly.

Dani wasn't hungry, but champagne on an empty stomach would make her giddy.

Several guests stopped to say hello and talk for a minute as she made her way to the food line. The band broke into their first number. Pierce and Grace stepped onto the dance floor that had been sprinkled with sawdust.

They looked incredibly happy. So perfect together that Dani's eyes grew moist.

She blinked and then spotted Riley and Tucker

standing near the dance floor surrounded by a different cluster of fawning women. No surprise there. It would be difficult to find three more hunky cowboys than the Lawrence brothers.

When she'd first spotted Riley in his tux, he literally took her breath away. Her pulse had gone into orbit as she walked the aisle. He looked even better now that he'd shed the stiff bow tie and donned his black Stetson.

She felt a touch to her arm and turned around. Millie Miles was standing at her elbow. Dani had met the woman while visiting Grace at the Double K Ranch a couple of months back and had run in to her in town and at the bakery several times since then.

The woman was always friendly, but there was no missing the sadness in her eyes. She'd recently lost her grandson, and her husband was in prison for manslaughter related to the tragic accident that had also claimed the toddler's life.

It was the kind of story you expected to see on TV, but never in a town like Winding Creek.

"I just wanted to say what a beautiful maid of honor you were," Millie said. "I love the dress. You should always wear that shade of green."

"Thanks. I'll certainly give that some consideration. Not sure how it would look with food-coloring stains, though," Dani joked. Compliments always tended to make her uncomfortable—unless they were in reference to her pastries.

"This is probably not the best time for this, but may I ask a favor of you?"

"Sure," Dani said.

"It's my daughter, Angela. She's the blonde in the red dress talking to Riley Lawrence."

"Yes, I've seen Angela in the shop with you."

Angela always dressed provocatively, but perhaps never looked as dynamite as she did tonight in the skintight dress with the revealing cutouts.

"What about Angela?"

"I don't know how much you know about our situation, but Angela's two-year-old son died in a freak accident last year. I won't go in to all the tragic details, but it has been extremely hard on Angela, as you might guess."

"I'm sure this is difficult for all of you."

Dani had no idea where this was going, but it didn't seem the time or place to discuss this.

"I'm increasingly worried about Angela," Millie said. "She seems to be in a state of denial, as if she refuses to believe any of the past actually happened."

Definitely not the time or place for this conversation. Dani had to agree that she didn't look like a grieving mother of a dead child, but… "I'm not the one you need to talk to about this."

"I know. I tend to go on once I get started. I was just hoping you could give her a job at the bakery."

"Does she want a job?" From what Dani had heard, the Mileses were wealthy enough that Angela wouldn't need the small salary Dani could pay her.

"She needs something to help settle her. A job that's not too complex but would force her to stay on a schedule and demonstrate a level of responsibility."

That didn't answer Dani's question. Or maybe it did. Millie was looking for an intervention for her daughter whether Angela wanted it or not.

"I don't think Dani's Delights fits her needs. It's very hectic at times. People expect good service and a smile."

Dani needed dependable help, but she wasn't a psychologist and had no experience dealing with serious emotional issues.

"If you'd just give her a chance."

Millie was pleading. Dani was still convinced it would be a mistake, but she didn't have the heart to say no with Millie looking as if she might start weeping at any second.

Dani let her gaze go back to Angela. The woman was animated, laughing, her hands now all over Tucker. Riley had disappeared, probably hijacked by some other hottie.

"I can't promise you anything," Dani said, "but have Angela come by and talk to me tomorrow afternoon around four. We close at three on Sunday, but I'll be around. Just tell her to ring the bell."

"Thank you. You won't be sorry."

Dani had a disturbing premonition that would not be the case, especially now, when her patience was being stretched to the limits by James Haggard.

Deep in thought as Millie walked away, she was

caught off guard when Riley came up behind her and put both hands on her shoulders. A traitorous tingle of awareness rushed her veins.

"You're not trying to avoid me, are you?" he asked.

"No, but you looked to be well cared for the last time I noticed."

"Tucker's fan club was spilling over. He puts out that virile, macho vibe that all bull riders do." Riley hooked an arm around her waist. "I think you owe me a dance."

"Then I guess we should get that over with," she teased in an effort to hide her pleasure that he'd remembered.

"You have a cruel side, you know that?"

"You can't expect every woman here to fall all over you."

He leaned close and whispered in her ear, "I'll settle for one."

In spite of her vows to be sensible, her insides melted as he led her onto the floor. He fit his arms around her and pulled her closer. Desire swelled to the point she could barely breathe, much less dance.

She was so lost in the moment that she didn't realize at first that Tucker was cutting in when he appeared over Riley's shoulder.

"You have to share this beauty, bro. *All* the best men get to dance with the maid of honor."

"Okay, but one time only," Riley said.

Dani tried to make conversation with Tucker, but

she was in such an emotional state, it was hard to pull off a simple sentence. She watched Riley leave the dance floor and return a minute later with not one but two adorable partners—Constance and Jaci.

He held both their hands and twirled them like some of the other couples were doing. They giggled and spun as if they were dancing queens.

That did it. The most she'd ever get out of Riley was a few heart-stopping moments, but she was ten tons of crazy about that man.

She had no plans to let him know that.

The rest of the evening was like a dream. Not that she danced every dance with Riley, but he was never gone from her side for long.

They were over three hours into the reception and many of the guests had left before she finally found herself totally alone with Riley near the back of the reception tent.

The band was playing a slow ballad and a lot of the remaining couples, along with Pierce and Grace, were dancing.

Constance and Jaci had finally run out of energy and had settled down with their iPads. Esther was sitting next to them, nodding and yawning.

"Looks like it's time for me to get Constance home," Dani said. "I'm sure Esther is ready to put Jaci and herself to bed even if the newlyweds party on."

Riley slipped an arm around her waist. "I was hoping we could escape and take a walk beneath the stars before you left."

Conflicting emotions sent her heart to her throat. His touch set her on fire, but what did he want from her. A kiss? A short fling before he moved on again? Or was this just the routine with a love-'em-and-leave-'em cowboy?

Not that she was actually looking for more. Getting the bakery on its feet and helping Constance adjust to her new life took practically every waking second.

And now there was James Haggard to add to the mix. There was no time for even a temporary romantic escapade in her life.

"I'll have to take a rain check on the walk. I really should take Constance home. This is well past her bedtime."

Riley slid his hand from around Dani's waist and took one of her hands in his. "You're not afraid of being alone with me, are you?"

"Should I be?"

"I'll never do anything you don't want me to do."

That wasn't a lot of reassurance. All she had to do was look into his eyes and her willpower would melt like butter on a hot cinnamon bun.

"I'm making you uncomfortable," he said. "That's not at all what I intended."

"It's not that," she lied. "But I do need to get home. I have a busy day tomorrow."

"You have to work on Sunday?"

"My boss is a slave driver."

"What time do you close the bakery?"

"Three on Sundays. Four every other day. Except

Monday. Then we're closed all day, but this week I may have business in San Antonio." If by a stroke of luck she could get a sample of James's DNA.

"Are you always this tough on a guy trying to get to know you better?"

"I have been accused of that before." More than once.

"I'm not giving up," Riley said. "What about dinner Monday night, or better yet, why don't you and Constance come back out to the ranch after you close tomorrow? We can explore the ranch on horseback or in my pickup truck. I need to reintroduce myself to the Double K."

She wanted to say yes, but her overly cautious nature held her back. Riley Lawrence was a heartache waiting to happen.

"I'll see. If not, perhaps one afternoon next week if that works for you. Constance doesn't have school Monday through Wednesday. Teacher workshops."

"How about both Sunday and a couple of afternoons next week? Every kid needs some time on a ranch."

"No promises, but I will try."

"And I'll keep thinking of you back in that kitchen creating all those delicious pastries. Spreading the creamy fillings. Dripping the caramel sauce. Licking the bowl."

A traitorous craving rippled through her body, a need so intense she had to fight the urge to wrap herself in his arms the way she had on the dance floor.

A walk with him in the moonlight would most definitely do her in.

"I really have to go now," she said, suddenly terrified by the strength of her feelings for a man she barely knew.

"Then let me drive you home," Riley persisted.

"I have my car here."

"But it's late. No reason for you and your niece to be out alone on these old country roads this time of night."

"It's Winding Creek," she reminded him. "I don't think there's any reason to worry."

"You drive a hard bargain, Dani Boatman."

She loved hearing her name on his lips. The name she'd had since birth, but it had never sounded erotic before.

"Dani."

She turned at Grace's frantic voice. An armed deputy with a dead serious expression on his face was walking at her side.

"What's wrong?" Riley asked.

The deputy looked past him and spoke directly to Dani. "There's been a break-in at your bakery."

She swallowed hard past a lump in her throat. "Are you sure? Sometimes the wind can set off the alarm system."

"There has definitely been a break-in and some damage. Deputies are on the scene. I can drive you there if you want."

"I'll drive her," Riley said.

Her first impulse was irritation that he took control, as if she couldn't handle this. But in truth she had no idea what she'd find when she got to the bakery and she didn't want to face it alone.

"Is there a problem?" Esther asked, joining them.

"My bakery has been broken into."

"Oh, mercy me. What is this world coming to? Did you catch the no-account bloke who did it?"

"Not yet," the deputy said, "but we will."

"Well, you can't do it soon enough to suit me. Terrible when a hardworking person can't even operate a business without someone stealing from her."

"Right about that," the deputy agreed.

"Why don't you just leave Constance here with me for the night?" Esther offered. "No use to drag her into that mess."

"I can't ask you to do that. You must be exhausted after all you've done today."

"You didn't ask. I offered. Besides, Constance isn't a bit of trouble. I figure she and Jaci will be so tired they'll fall asleep the second their heads hit the pillows. I'm sure I can find a cotton T-shirt she can sleep in."

"She should definitely stay," Grace said. "Pierce and I aren't leaving for San Antonio until tomorrow morning. I can help with the girls tonight."

"You're on your honeymoon."

"I've been on a honeymoon since the day I met Pierce. Helping get the girls to bed won't change that."

"It's settled," Esther said.

This time Dani didn't argue. "Thanks. I appreciate this more than you know. Constance bought her backpack with her, so she has her favorite doll and some books. She changed into her wedding finery after we got here, so she can put on the jeans and shirt she was wearing earlier when she gets up in the morning."

Grace put her arm around Dani's waist. "Don't worry about her.

"Riley, you take care of Dani," Esther ordered.

"I plan to."

He took her arm protectively as they followed the deputy back toward the house where he'd parked his squad car. Dread clawed at the lining of Dani's stomach as they made the drive into town.

The bakery wasn't just a shop. It was her livelihood. Her home. Constance's home, the place where Dani always wanted her to feel safe.

The first thing she saw when they turned onto Main Street was a squad car and the sheriff's vehicle in front of her shop, blue lights flashing. A cluster of strangers stood on the opposite side of the street observing the action.

The second the car stopped, she jumped out and rushed to the open door of the shop. Anger erupted at the havoc she faced. The feeling was so fierce, her insides seemed to explode.

She didn't have to wonder what had happened here. No one ever broke into the shops in this area.

James Haggard had returned, just as he'd promised he would. Only he hadn't waited a week. He'd barely backed off for twenty-four hours.

If it was hardball he wanted, he'd get it.

## Chapter Five

The intense odor of coffee sent Dani into an immediate coughing fit. A black film covered every surface and hung thick in the air. Two giant-sized canisters of coffee she had ground for the morning rush lay empty on the floor in front of the counter.

She braced herself against the display case as she scanned the rest of the destruction. It looked as if a tornado had blown through the shop and literally picked up everything and sent it crashing back to the tile floor.

Tables and chairs were overturned. Pastry cookbooks and coffee-themed gift items normally shelved along the side walls had been knocked to the floor, many cracked or shattered. Both cash-register drawers were open.

She had a crazy urge to pick up one of the chairs and hurl it as hard as she could against the wall, or to start screaming and pull out her hair. Fortunately, since she wasn't two years old, she refrained from doing what came naturally. She took a deep breath and managed a small measure of composure.

A deputy rushed in from the kitchen area. "This is a crime scene. No trespassing."

"I'm Dani Boatman. I own Dani's Delights, at least what's left of it. And this is my friend Riley Lawrence."

"Sorry, but I'll need to see some ID."

Sheriff Cavazos joined them from the back of the shop. "She doesn't need any ID. I'll vouch for her and her friend." He put out a hand to Riley. "I'm Sheriff Cavazos. We haven't met, but I know your brother Pierce and have known Esther Kavanaugh for years."

They exchanged handshakes.

"Sorry we're meeting under such down-and-dirty circumstances," Cavazos said. "Glad you're here to offer Dani some moral support. Always tough seeing your business trashed like this."

Dani picked up and righted an overturned chair that blocked her path. "I'm not sure I can stomach looking at the rest of the place."

"Fortunately, this is the worst of it," Sheriff Cavazos said. "There's no sign of damage in your fancy kitchen. Not even a scratch on those giant ovens. All your cinnamon-roll fans will be thankful for that. Me included."

"What about the upstairs living area?" Riley asked.

Dani held her breath, her stomach churning as she

waited for his response. If Haggard had been in Constance's room—if he'd handled any of her things...

"Untouched as far as we can tell," Cavazos said. "And believe me, we gave it a thorough check. Had to make sure the culprit wasn't hiding up there."

Dani shuddered. She hadn't even thought of that. She scanned the area again. "How did he get in?"

"Through the back door that opens to the alley. He broke the lock."

"So you think this was all done by one person?" Riley asked.

"I checked the area myself and only saw one set of fresh footprints in the patch of dirt between the door and the alleyway. Big feet. Definitely an adult male. Not wearing Western boots like so many around here do. Prints indicated he was wearing sneakers, no doubt looking for a fast getaway."

"So no eyewitness?" Riley asked.

"Nope." Cavazos raked his fingers through his thinning hair. "But we couldn't have missed the scoundrel by much. He busted the hell out of the system keypad next to the back door, but not before the call went through to the security company.

"When the company couldn't reach you, Dani, they called us."

"I was at the Double K for the wedding reception. Evidently I couldn't hear the phone over the band."

"Wouldn't have changed the results if you had. The first two deputies were on the scene in under five minutes. Your burglar wasted no time wrecking the place."

"Any suspects?" Riley asked. "Is this a pattern of similar vandalism and break-ins in Winding Creek?"

Cavazos shook his head and scratched his whiskered chin. "Last downtown business break-in we had was dang near three years ago. Then it was a couple of teenagers camping out down at the park on Winding Creek. They got high and hit Caffe's Bar looking for booze. Didn't make a mess like this, though."

"Your registers were emptied of all the bills," one of the deputies said. "That was probably the intruder's first order of business."

"That didn't gain him much. There was very little money in them. I emptied them when I closed shop for the day, except for enough bills and change to start business in the morning. Not that I'll be opening to customers tomorrow now."

"What about the cash you took in this morning?" Riley asked. "Where's that money?"

"I made a deposit at the drive-through lane before the bank closed. The rest is in a hidden safe upstairs."

"That might be your motivation for the vandalism," Cavazos said. "Jackass went for the cash and when there wasn't enough to satisfy him, he got pissed and did as much damage as he could before he heard the approaching sirens."

"Guess I'm lucky you got here so fast," she said. But she felt certain that wasn't the motivation for the vandalism. The culprit was that rotten James Haggard. He was devoid of any decency. A scoundrel who was determined to steal the trust fund of a motherless girl he claimed was his own flesh and blood.

Riley took off the jacket to his tux and wrapped it about her shoulders. That was when she realized she was trembling.

"I know you've got a major clean-up job here," he said. "The good news is there's very little costly damage. The best news is neither you nor Constance was home at the time of the break-in."

"I agree," she said. She wasn't sure if Haggard had only come by to threaten her again and then decided to break in when she wasn't here, or if vandalism had been his goal.

"I wouldn't advise you to try and stay here tonight," Cavazos said. "The lock on the back door is busted. Fact is, the whole door is busted up. It will have to be replaced, and it will likely be Monday before you can get someone out to take care of that for you."

"I'll secure it until the door's replaced," Riley said. "And I'll replace all the locks once the door is in, just to be on the safe side."

"Good idea," Cavazos said. "Now if you two will excuse me, I need to return a phone call. The deputies will be finishing up here in a few minutes. After that, the place is yours, but if you think of anything

I should know about, give me a call on my private line."

He handed them each a business card. He spoke briefly to his deputies and then left through the front door.

Dani's mind was reeling. Cleanup seemed all but insurmountable and she wasn't sure she had the strength or willpower to even start on it tonight.

And then there was Riley. She'd known him one day, yet he'd taken over tonight as if they were life-long friends—or more. He was protective, and far more clearheaded than she was at the moment.

He was both of those things now, but he could be gone tomorrow. She couldn't start depending on him.

"You don't have to stay tonight, Riley. Really, you've done so much already. I'm starting to feel guilty about taking up all your time when you're in Winding Creek to visit your brothers and Esther."

He looked puzzled. "Do you have a problem with my being here?"

"Of course not, but—"

"Then drop the guilt talk. No cowboy worth his boots would ever walk away from a woman in distress. Especially one who can bake the way you do," he added teasingly.

He smiled and suddenly she was unable to tear her gaze from him. He was still in his tux but seemingly as relaxed as if he was wearing his favorite jeans.

He was undoubtedly the most intriguing and se-

ductive man she'd ever met. Not pretty-boy hand-
some, but rugged and masculine, with eyes the color
of dark chocolate, thick locks of deep brown hair
that fell devilishly onto his forehead and a smile that
could melt glacial ice.

"I love you in that dress," he said, "but I'm not
sure it will ever come clean if it keeps collecting coffee grinds. And I'm damn sure that staying in this
monkey suit for much longer will stop the blood flow
to my brain—and other parts."

Her lustful thoughts cooled as she looked down
at her once beautiful dress. It looked as she'd been
caught in a whirlwind of black sand.

"So much for ever wearing this again," she said.
"I'm going upstairs and change. I'm afraid I don't
have anything in your size to offer you."

"No problem. I look terrible in feminine attire
anyway. Do you want me to go upstairs with you,
give the area another look around?"

"No, but if I run in to any unpleasant surprises,
I'll yell."

"And I'll come running."

That might be the first time a man had ever said
that to her. Fortunately there were no surprises waiting at the top of the stairs. The living area looked
exactly as she'd left it.

She peeked into Constance's room. Also untouched. She breathed easier. The thought of Hag-

gard handling any of Constance's possessions would have made her physically ill.

She headed straight for the shower, peeling off her clothes as she walked. Hot water and soap couldn't wash away the feeling she'd been sprayed with Haggard's special brand of poison, but at least she'd be more comfortable.

All of this would be far more traumatic if she was facing it alone. She wished she dared tell Riley about James Haggard, but she couldn't lay this on him.

Haggard was her responsibility and she couldn't afford a mistake. If there was one, Constance, in all her innocence, would be the one to pay.

RILEY WENT TO check out the back door while the deputies finished with their investigation of the crime scene. One was taking snapshots. The other was collecting fingerprints from the cash register.

True to the sheriff's report, the solid wooden door was a disaster. It hung from one hinge, open enough that a man could squeeze past it to get in and out of the shop. The top half of the door had a huge hole in it, as if someone very strong had slammed his fist through it. The bottom half was splintered.

Riley squeezed through the opening. There were no lights in the area, but the moon was bright enough that he could get a fair take on his surroundings.

The door opened onto a covering of dirt that bordered the alley. Three huge trash cans sat just to the right of the door. There was a fenced-in area about four feet deep that ran nearly the length of the building on the left. The gate to it had a latch but not a lock.

He walked over and peeked inside. Two air-conditioner units were housed there. A couple of empty clay flowerpots sat next to them beside a half-empty sack of pottery soil.

He stepped into the alley and scanned the rest of the area. Except for a couple of cats, Riley was the only sign of life.

It made sense a man would come in the back way if he was sneaking around. Chances were slim that he'd be noticed after dark—unless he set off an alarm system.

Riley suspected all stores had alarm systems these days, even in Winding Creek. The burglar should have expected that.

So why risk getting caught or possibly shot to break in to a bakery? It wasn't like there was anything that could be sold at the pawnshop for ready cash. So was it desperation, stupidity or a personal grudge against Dani?

She didn't seem the type to make enemies, but she was relatively new in town. Perhaps it was her past that was coming back to haunt her.

He reached for his phone and punched in Tucker's number.

"About time you called," Tucker said. "If I didn't hear from you by the time I finished loading these chairs on the back of the truck, I was planning to drive into town and see for myself what's going on."

"Loading chairs? Does that mean the guests have all left?"

"For the most part. The bride and groom have already been showered with birdseed and good wishes and escaped to their bedroom in the big house. And the band finished its last set about ten minutes ago. So what's up with the bakery?"

Riley filled him in as succinctly as possible.

"Poor Dani. She must be freaking out."

"All in all, she's handling it pretty well."

"What can I do to help?"

"Bring me some lumber—a few sheets of plywood and some two-by-fours if Esther has some lying around the ranch."

"You need all of that tonight?"

"Yep. I need to board up the back door until she can get it replaced. Can't even close it now, much less secure it."

"What about tools?"

"I've probably got all I need in my truck. But I need some jeans and a shirt. Got to get out of this tux before it strangles me."

"I get that. I've already changed back into jeans myself. Does this mean you're going to start cleaning tonight?"

"Not if I can help it. Tomorrow's soon enough for me, but I figure I'll spend the night here and help

Dani get an early start on tackling the rubble remains tomorrow."

"Spend the night? Really? Am I missing something here?"

"Just living by the code, bro. Gotta protect the women."

"And, of course, it doesn't hurt if they're cute. Lumber and a change of clothes. Anything else?"

"That should do it."

"I'll be there as soon as I can break free here. That shouldn't take long."

"Appreciate it."

"No problem," Tucker said. "Who knew Winding Creek would be this exciting?"

Certainly not Riley. And to think he'd been wasting his time with a bunch of cows.

# Chapter Six

James Haggard stood on the bank of Winding Creek beneath the shadowed branches of an ancient oak tree. The moon was so bright he could see three deer at the edge of the woods on the opposite bank. An owl hooted and somewhere in the distance he heard the howl of coyotes.

In another situation, he might have appreciated the setting. Tonight he felt nothing but the desperation roaring through his veins like a runaway freight train.

He'd seen his daughter for the first time yesterday. It hadn't been planned. He'd been sitting in the back of Dani's Delights, sipping a coffee and sizing up Dani Boatman as an adversary.

It was after three when the door opened and a freckle-faced girl, her hair in braids, swung through the door, a huge smile on her face. She was friendly and full of life the way her mother had been in the old days.

Memories of Amber had flooded his mind. She'd

been so beautiful and loving. When they made love, he had felt he was the luckiest man in the world. He'd have done anything she'd asked him to do.

He had even almost gotten shot once while robbing a liquor store to keep her in the fancy rehab center while she was pregnant with Constance.

His woman and his child. He hadn't wanted to steal, but he couldn't let them down.

The rehab had never taken root. After Constance was born, Amber had hit the drugs harder than ever. Eventually, she'd kicked James out of her life.

But she'd loved him. He knew she had. It was the drugs and other men who'd torn her away from him.

He'd half expected to feel some instinctive connection with Constance when he saw her. Nothing clicked. All he could think of was Amber and the way she'd used him when all he'd wanted to do was take care of her.

But this wasn't about Constance. This was what was owed him. He was Constance's father. By rights the insurance settlement should have been his. All he wanted was his rightful share.

Tonight had been a near catastrophe. He'd lost his cool, let the situation lead to uncontrolled rage. He'd always had a problem with that, more so lately than ever before.

But tonight's episode had gained him nothing. He'd been barely inside, trying to decide where to start searching for Constance's birth certificate, when he heard the approaching sirens.

The birth certificate would prove he was the father. He knew it and Dani knew it, no matter what she claimed.

Frustrated, he'd given in to rage, wrecking what he could before escaping out the back door as men with guns raced inside through the front.

At least Dani would know he meant business now.

Red drops of blood plopped onto his shoe.

Damn. His hand had begun to bleed again. He turned and headed back inside the cheap rental cabin for another makeshift bandage and a glass of whiskey to dull the pain.

This had been a damn rotten night.

## Chapter Seven

Dani turned on the vacuum cleaner but then just stood staring at the mess that faced her. She'd been so proud of her shop, thrilled that the future in Winding Creek had felt so promising for her and Constance.

The senseless destruction created an empty feeling inside her, as if it was a harbinger of things to come. It was exasperating how much pain one greedy, vengeful man could spawn, just for the sake of proving to her that he had no boundaries when it came to getting what he wanted.

But he would soon find out she had no boundaries when it came to keeping Constance safe.

She vacuumed and then mopped a swath down the middle of the shop to at least provide a clean walkway. It was only a start but all she felt like tackling tonight.

Tucker and Riley were probably just as fatigued as she was after the long day, but she could hear the hum of the saws and the pounding of the hammers as the men boarded up the back door.

She stopped at the pile of broken items around the nearly empty shelves. She picked up a delicate teapot, one of her favorite purchases from her last trip to market. The handle was missing and there was a chip at the spout. It would have to be trashed. Still, she carefully placed what was left on it back on the shelf for now.

That was when she noticed the smeared crimson dots along the edge of one of the shelves. She visually followed the trail of stain to a mound of broken glass. Drops of blood, not quite dry, glistened on what had once been an etched trifle bowl.

The glass was mostly shards except for one larger curved piece of the bowl. At least a tablespoon of blood had pooled in the curved remains.

Her heart jumped to her throat. That had to be James Haggard's blood. His DNA. Right at her fingertips.

Excitement trilled through her. Luck might just have taken a swift turn in her direction. Unfortunately, she didn't have the sterile container the kit would provide.

She considered her options. A plastic ziplock bag would have to do.

She hurried to the kitchen for the bag and a pair of protective gloves. Afraid of spilling even a drop, she gingerly tipped the piece of glass so that the blood flowed into the bag.

She wrapped the bag in the same white paper she

used to line boxes of pastry and then slid it to the seldom-used top shelf in her bakeware pantry.

Now it was just a matter of waiting. According to information at the website, results would be ready in three to five days by phone after the DNA was in their hands and the written document would arrive by mail a workday or two later.

Dani would see that the samples were at the Corinthian Court Lab by Monday afternoon.

A happy ending for everyone except Haggard—as long as the DNA proved his threats were nothing but a scam. Right now she had to think positively about that.

DEAD TIRED BUT with the back door to the bakery secured, Riley adjusted the spray so that it was as hot as he could stand it. He liked his showers *caliente*, his salsa *picantes* and his life uncomplicated. He hadn't even been in Winding Creek twenty-four hours yet and his life was as complicated as it had ever been.

He was feeling a bit like he'd blown into town on a hurricane and dropped into a stampede of wild horses. Only wild horses might not have been nearly as disruptive to his life as Dani Boatman.

Sure, she was cute, smart and witty, but that didn't fully explain the instantaneous attraction to her from the moment he'd walked into Dani's Delights. Kind of like a bite of one of her famous cinnamon rolls that, if he could believe all the comments he'd heard this morning, left everyone wanting more.

Riley was yet to taste one of those rolls, but he'd known immediately he wanted to get to know her better. He'd never expected to be standing naked in her shower tonight—albeit alone.

Not that he could chalk up that development to his irresistible charm. He owed his being here tonight to the jerk who'd wrecked her bakery. Crazy timing for sure, for a town that seldom saw this type of senseless crime.

A random attack or was the bakery targeted? If it was the latter, what would have happened if the alarm hadn't gone off or if Dani had been in the shop's kitchen when the son of a bitch busted through the door?

What if he came back when she and Constance were here alone?

Those troubling thoughts kicked around in Riley's mind as he soaped his body and shampooed his hair.

The back door to the shop was boarded over for now, but Riley planned to replace it with one reinforced with iron bars that would be a lot more difficult to break through. He'd checked the front door. It needed better and more secure locks, as well.

But no matter how secure the doors were, the huge display window would always be an easy point of entry. The best he could do with that was encourage her to make sure her replacement alarm system was top-of-the-line.

He had the next few days' work cut out for him—as long as she let him keep hanging around.

He stepped out of the shower and grabbed a thick, sky-blue towel from the rack. The towel was slightly damp and smelled of the same intoxicating scent that clung to Dani. He'd never taken much notice of fragrances before, but tonight even that was a turn-on.

A competing odor grabbed his attention—a whiff of bacon made his mouth water and his stomach grumble. It occurred to him as he yanked on his jeans that he'd had nothing to eat tonight except a couple of bites of stuffed quail appetizers.

He'd skipped the other reception food, partly because he was more interested in enjoying Dani's company. Admittedly, also because of the fabulous noon meal Esther had on the table when he'd finally arrived at the Double K Ranch after leaving the bakery.

He and his brothers had chastised her for cooking for them when she was so busy with wedding preparations. She'd claimed cooking was her balm when things got hectic.

Maybe that was true of Dani, too. Perhaps she was in her commercial kitchen, pounding and shaping dough or measuring ingredients for her next creation.

But he wasn't familiar with any pastries that smelled like bacon. He headed downstairs without bothering with shoes or a shirt.

Dani was cutting dough into triangles, so absorbed in what she was doing she didn't even notice when he joined her. He stared appreciatively.

She was in faded jeans, the interesting kind with authentic rips in suggestive, though not indecent, places.

Nice hips. Even nicer ass. No red-blooded cowboy under ninety could fail to appreciate that. He struggled to resist walking over and fitting his hands around the tempting buttocks.

"What are you making?" he asked.

She spun around.

"Didn't mean to startle you."

"Not your fault. My nerves are still a bit on edge. I'm making stuffed breakfast croissants. Hope you're hungry. They'll be ready in about twenty minutes."

"I'm starved. Can I help?"

"Sure. You're in charge of the bacon. When it's nice and crispy, lay the strips on the paper towels I spread out on the counter. Once they cool enough to handle, crumble them in bite-size pieces."

"Got it." Her hands seemed to fly as she poured heavy cream into a bowl and added a generous sprinkle of powdered sugar. Using a hand-held electric mixer, she whipped the cream into mounds of fluff.

"What are we going to do with the whipped cream?"

"You'll see," Dani promised. She dipped one finger into the bowl and then held it to his lips.

He sucked and swallowed the gooey sweetness while his imagination went on a wild ride. His appetite switched gears. Now it was Dani he was hungry for.

She went right back to the task at hand, cracking large brown eggs into another bowl. This time she used a fork to beat them until they were the color of lemons and smooth as silk.

He was so mesmerized by her graceful, competent movements that he almost let the bacon burn. He forked it quickly onto the paper towels and turned off the gas.

His ravenous desire for her was as sizzling as the bacon had been. He wasn't exactly getting those same vibes from her, but he couldn't help visualizing what those long, mesmerizing fingers of hers could do to him.

Unless… "Is there a significant other in your life?" he asked as she scrambled the eggs.

"You mean besides Constance, who pretty much rules the roost?"

"Yeah. Some guy you're crazy about who's got you all wrapped up and off the market."

She laughed softly and shook her head. "I'm not sure I was ever really *on the market*, as you put it."

"Why not?"

"I'm a born workaholic. I haven't had a date since Constance came to live with me eight months ago. Tonight's the first time I've danced since the last wedding I attended, and that was over a year ago."

"We'll have to remedy that."

"That would be fun, except that my time for a social life is extremely limited these days."

"I'm starting to think you have something against cowboys."

"Absolutely not. If I did, you'd be getting stale muffins tonight instead of my croissant specialty."

She folded the eggs into the whipped cream while he crumbled the bacon. Next, she spooned the egg mixture across the widest part of the doughy triangles and then sprinkled it with the bacon and grated cheese.

She reached down and grabbed a scoop of flour from somewhere and sprinkled it on the work surface.

"Are you also a magician? It looked like you just pulled that flour from thin air."

"No, but I indulged big for my super-convenient flour-canister drawers. Close the drawer and a built-in cover keeps the flour dry and clean. Open the drawer with a foot control and the canister is open, the flour ready to scoop or measure without my touching sticky or floured hands on clean surfaces."

"Who knew being a pastry chef required so many expensive gadgets?"

"The salespeople who make a living convincing us we need them."

He watched her roll the first one and then joined in, rolling one in the same time it took her to finish the other four. In minutes she'd slid six filled croissants into a hot oven.

"This is guaranteed to be the fanciest midnight snack I ever had," he said. "Of course, you're only competing with a glass of milk and store-bought cookies."

"Store-bought cookies. Wash your mouth out with soap."

"Hate the taste of soap. Do you have any wine?"

"No, but there are a few beers in the larger refrigerator that I keep for when Grace and Pierce come to dinner."

"That's even better."

He retrieved two beers, opened both of them and slid one across the worktable next to where Dani was arranging raspberries and strawberries on two white plates she'd decorated with swirls of chocolate sauce. He felt like he'd crashed a TV cooking show.

As Riley sipped his beer, his mind tripped back to his earlier concerns that she was a target. "I know you said that you had no idea who broke in to the shop."

"I don't," she answered quickly.

"I just thought that since you've had time to think of it, a suspect might have come to mind. Perhaps some jerk who wants to get back at you for some real or perceived injustice?"

She visibly tensed. "No. I've made no enemies since moving here."

"What about before you moved to Winding Creek? A disgruntled employer? A vicious neighbor? Some guy you dumped and broke his heart?"

"No. No one. Look, I don't want to talk about this anymore tonight. I don't even want to think about it."

The conversation had definitely upset her. Her hands shook as she yanked the pan of croissants from the oven and set them down hard on a cooling rack.

All convincing signs she was lying. He had a strong hunch that she knew who'd broken in and was afraid to say. But why? To protect the intruder? Or to protect herself or Constance?

She pushed his filled plate across the counter to him. "You know, now that the back door is secured, there's really no reason for you to stay overnight. You should go home after we eat and get some rest. You're here to see your family and Esther, not to babysit the chef."

"Let me worry about that." He reached across the work surface and covered her hands with his. "If you're having problems, you can trust me, Dani. I'm one of the good guys. Texas roots. Cowboy code. All that and a plate of tacos."

"I am leveling with you."

"Doesn't feel that way."

She pulled her hands away. "It's just been a long day—for both of us. You surely need a break from rescue duties."

She'd tried to lighten her tone, but it wasn't quite working. Riley trailed a finger from her shoulder to her chin and tilted it so that she had to meet his gaze. "Do you want me to go, Dani?"

She sighed and took a deep breath, as if trying to come to grips with her own feelings.

"I'd like you to stay," she murmured. "Just no more talk tonight of the break-in."

"You got it."

"Now let's eat," she said, "before your most-elegant-ever midnight snack gets cold."

He wouldn't push anymore right now, but he wasn't letting this go, either. Not just because she'd crawled under his skin and stirred desire on every level. She might need his help, even if she was too stubborn to admit it.

A few seconds later he bit into the golden, flaky croissant. The warm creamy eggs and crispy bacon filling flooded his mouth and created a heaven for his taste buds.

"What do you think?" Dani asked once he'd swallowed and licked his lips.

"Wow. Will you marry me?" he said, not sure at that exact moment that he was teasing.

"Depends on what kind of job you do on the back door," she teased.

The tension had passed, at least on the surface. But the issue of her safety was far from over. Somehow he had to win her trust.

Which translated to the fact that he'd best control his manly urges. No trying to jump her bones tonight.

DANI WOKE WITH a start, jerking to a sitting position, her mind wedged between nightmare and reality. She shivered, slowly realizing that her cotton nightshirt was soaked in cold sweat.

Even as the dregs of sleep faded, the nightmare continued to stalk the edge of her consciousness. She'd been reaching for Constance, trying to save her before she backed off a craggy ledge. But no matter how close Dani got, Constance remained just out of reach.

Dani hugged her knees to her chest as her eyes adjusted to the dim moonlight squeezing through the blinds and striping the shadowed walls. The terrifying sense of helplessness wouldn't let go.

She was in Constance's room, having insisted Riley, with his much larger frame, sleep in her king-size bed. His being here seemed right on so many levels but wrong on just as many others. He'd come to her rescue without hesitation, taken control, flirted just enough to make her feel feminine and desirable. Mostly he'd made her feel safe tonight.

The nightmare had been a horrifying reminder that locks and reinforced doors couldn't keep her and Constance safe from James Haggard. If he was Constance's biological father, there was a heartbreaking chance that he could gain custody of her.

*Amber, how could you have created such a marvelous daughter with a heartless monster like Haggard?*

Dani kicked away the covers, crawled from between the sheets and padded to the window. Gathering the hem of her nightshirt between her fingers, she pulled the damp shirt over her head and dropped it to the floor. The pulsing fear of the nightmare settled into an uneasy drumming of her nerves.

She'd feel better if she could hear Constance's voice and know that she was safe. She glanced at the clock—3:00 a.m. She'd only upset everyone in Esther's household if she called now.

But unless she was wrong about Haggard's being the one who broke in to her shop, she'd soon know if he was Constance's biological father, as he claimed.

If it turned out that he was…

She couldn't even go there. All she knew was that as long as she had enough breath to fight, he would never get custody of Constance.

Dawn crept back through the windows before she fell asleep again.

DANI MEASURED THE square of poster board, making marks to ensure that her sign was symmetrical and at least semiprofessional-looking. She wanted it on the door before she tackled the clean-up job.

"Want a refill?" Riley asked as he picked up his empty mug.

"Not until I finish this. I don't want to risk dripping coffee on my work of art. But could you bring me my phone off the counter? I called Esther about thirty minutes ago to check on Constance, and she hasn't called me back."

"They're probably all involved with seeing off Grace and Pierce. Two days is a lousy honeymoon, but I can see why they're putting off their trip to Italy until July. Spring on any ranch is a hectic time."

"So I've heard. Before moving here, I'd never been on a ranch."

"But you do ride horses?"

"I have ridden a few times, mostly since I started spending a little time with Grace at the Double K. I wouldn't say I ride."

"Honey, we have a lot of work to do in a short time. What about Constance? Does she know how to ride?"

A short time. At least he wasn't pretending he was interested in long-term commitment.

"Pierce has been giving Constance riding lessons every Wednesday afternoon. She loves it."

"You can't let her show you up." Riley looked over her shoulder as she started printing. "You know you could just leave the sign that's already on the door turned to closed instead of wasting so much time constructing a new one."

"Not in a town the size of Winding Creek. The regulars know I'm supposed to open at ten on Sundays. If I don't provide at least a minimal explanation, they'll be banging on the locked door trying to make sure I'm okay."

"Checking up on their favorite pastry chef." He refilled his mug and grabbed another warm morning glory muffin from the basket next to the coffeepot. "So, what explanation are you giving them?"

"Closed today for personal emergency."

"Oh, yeah, like that won't get the gossip mills grinding."

"I know, but everyone in town will know about the break-in before the day is over. I just don't want them bothering me while I'm cleaning, especially since I won't be dressed for company."

"When do you plan to reopen?"

"Tuesday morning at my usual time of seven."

"Why not take the whole week off? It's a shame to spend all this beautiful spring inside."

"I can't take off. This is a business. I already have orders for two birthday cakes, petits fours for a bridal shower and filled croissants for a ladies auxiliary committee meeting on Friday night. I can't just toss my responsibilities aside."

"Right." He put up a hand to stop her arguments. "The workaholic's creed."

"That's not it."

Oh, who was she kidding? She hadn't had a real vacation in over a year. Constance was out of school until Thursday. A couple of days off would give them time to have fun together.

Dani couldn't take a week off, but her business wouldn't fall apart if she was closed a couple of extra days.

"Maybe I will take Tuesday and Wednesday off," she said.

"What about your birthday cakes and petit fours?"

"Actually only one of the cakes is due before I'd reopen on Thursday—a birthday cake for Myrtle Higgins's ninety-year-old mother. I'll give Myrtle a call and assure her I'll have it ready whenever she wants to pick it up."

"I like this spontaneous you."

"Now I just have to decide how Constance and I will spend our unexpected mini-vacation."

"I know the perfect place. Close by. Free room and board in a homey ranch house. Wide-open spaces. Fishing. Horseback riding. Picnics by a creek. Roasting hot dogs over a campfire under the stars—with a personal guitar strummer if that's your fancy.

"Best food in nine counties—besides yours, of course. And a personal entertainment guide, guaranteed to please."

"Sounds like an offer too good to refuse."

"Then my job is done. I'll call Esther and tell her to expect two more guests. She'll be thrilled. The more people she can feed, the happier she is."

"Only for Tuesday and Wednesday," Dani said, "if that's actually okay with Esther."

"It's a deal."

It would be a perfect vacation for Constance, who could never get enough of the ranch—Esther was always inviting her out for a few days. And it would mean she could likely avoid James Haggard until after she had the paternity testing results.

There was only one drawback with Riley's plan.

He would be the guide guaranteed to please. Love-'em-and-leave-'em Riley Lawrence.

She hated to even think of the hearts he'd left broken in his wake. If she wasn't very careful, she'd be the latest.

"I have just one question," she said.

"Ask away."

"Why do you want me at the Double K Ranch? You have your brothers, Esther and an adorable niece of your own to get to know. Why are you bothering with a headache and a half like me?"

He smiled, the boyish grin that rocked her heart. "I wish I knew, Dani Boatman. I wish to hell I knew. But I'm just a cowboy. Long as I've got a good horse and a decent saddle, I don't question fate."

# Chapter Eight

The relief Dani felt after talking to Esther and Constance gave her just the energy jolt she needed to get to down to the serious work of cleaning up.

She ripped through her closet, looking for something old and worn enough she wouldn't mind if it bit the dust during the cleaning process. She pulled out a plastic storage container of clothes that she'd worn for working in her postage-stamp-size yard before moving to Winding Creek.

Rummaging through the oldies, she pulled out a pair of faded jean cutoffs. If she could squeeze into them, they'd be perfect for scrubbing floors. She checked the size label as she stepped into them. Size ten.

She snapped and zipped them easily. If anything they were too loose. Nothing sexy about loose denim, but she was thrilled to be losing a little weight.

Besides, if Riley was looking for sexy model types, he'd have to go find one of the hotties who had been hanging on to him at the reception.

Dani couldn't compete with them and wouldn't try.

Grabbing a gray, slightly-stained T-shirt, she pulled it on, yanking it down to fit around her hips. She slipped her bright-blue polished toes into a pair of flip-flops and checked her appearance in the closet mirror.

Gross.

She ran a brush through the mass of tight curls that hugged her neck and cheeks, a move that did little to tame them. A quick brush of lipstick and she'd have to do.

The front doorbell was ringing as she headed down the stairs, followed by what sounded like a fist pounding on the wood. Adrenaline flooded her veins.

Surely Haggard had better sense than to show up here before the vandalism he'd caused was even cleaned up.

She heard the door open.

"Help has arrived. Let the fun begin!"

It was Tucker, in running shorts and an Oklahoma State T-shirt. "Good morning, gorgeous," he said, giving her a peck on the cheek.

Nice-looking guy. Friendly and funny. So why didn't her heart skip beats when he touched her?

"You're out and about early," she said.

"I figured you could use an extra pair of hands this morning."

"Yes, we can."

"Before I forget, Esther said to tell you that she was taking the girls to Sunday school and church and then to the spring festival and students' rodeo at the high school. She said if that's a problem, let her know. Otherwise, they'll see you later today."

"Not a problem. She mentioned that they might do that when she returned my call earlier this morning. I'd like to have this place back to near-normal before Constance sees it. I can't keep the break-in from her. There are no secrets in Winding Creek, but I don't want to frighten her."

"Hopefully this will be over and done before she has time to give it much thought. The sheriff will likely have the jerk in jail before the day is over," Tucker said. "Chances are he's already got a good idea who's responsible."

Dani doubted that.

"Did you go shopping?" Riley asked, joining them from upstairs and spying the two large brown bags Tucker had brought in with him.

"No. I raided Esther's supply closet. Figured we might need these." He pulled out a half-gallon bottle of bleach, two large bottles of household cleansers and a half-dozen sponges.

"There's more where these come from. I never realized Esther was such a hoarder, but she has enough assorted household gadgets, jars and cleansers in that closet off the laundry room to supply half the town."

"Hopefully we won't need all this," Dani said, "but then again we might."

Riley looked in the other bag and lifted out two

six packs of beer. "Now we're getting down to the real necessities."

"Brewskies before noon?" Dani asked teasingly.

"It's five o'clock somewhere," Riley quipped.

"I also went through your things and discovered a pair of jeans that looked as if you might have worn them to a fight with a wildcat," Tucker said. "Figured if you accidentally splashed bleach on them, it would be an improvement.

Riley held up the jeans. "These are my favorite. You have no appreciation for style."

Tucker folded the emptied brown bags. "So, where do we start, boss lady?"

She loved his attitude.

"If we're not careful, we'll be getting in each other's way all day," she said.

"Agreed," Riley said. "I say Tucker and I tackle the jobs that only require elbow grease and leave the ones that require expertise to you."

Dani went to the counter and grabbed a pad and pen. "We need to clean the floor first. Then all the counters and display cases should be cleaned." She looked around the room. "Even the light fixtures and fans are black."

"What about all the stuff that was on the shelves?" Riley asked. "Some of that will have to be trashed, but some is hopefully salvageable."

"Yes," Dani agreed. "And everything that's trashed will have to be listed and reported to the insurance company." She quickly scribbled down the tasks. "Pick your poison, gentlemen."

"I'll tackle the floors with the vacuum to start with," Tucker offered.

"I'll follow him with a mop," Riley said. "And if you don't mind taking a suggestion from a mere mop maid, you should work on the gift items, Dani."

And they were off. It took her a few minutes to get organized. Just as she started actually sorting the items, Riley returned from changing clothes. He was shirtless and barefoot. The well-worn jeans were snapped just below the waist.

A scattering of dark hairs sprinkled his chest, some curling around his nipples. The hair narrowed into a triangle that disappeared inside the zipper of the faded denim.

Lean. Muscular. Mouthwatering.

She looked like a homeless woman. He looked like a Greek god. No. He looked like a cowboy. A hunky, gorgeous, authentic cowboy.

She struggled to tear her gaze from him before she gave in to the ravenous temptation to trail her fingers down his bare abdomen.

She counted to ten silently and hoped the sensible, controlled workaholic that never melted into unadulterated lust would reappear. It didn't work.

Riley turned on the radio and found a country music station. He and Tucker joined in on half the songs as they worked, Riley actually in key.

When the floors were done, Tucker popped the

top on some beers and handed her one. She stood and stretched, then massaged her neck with her fingers.

Riley walked over, stopped behind her and took over the neck-rub duties. His thumbs put pressure in all the right spots to ease the muscle fatigue. His fingers were gentle on her skin, brushing her earlobes, then tangling in the wild, curly locks of her hair.

Her pulse soared until she was giddy with emotions that she could neither understand nor control.

A new song started on the radio, an old classic… slow, mellow. Riley tugged her around to face him and pulled her into his arms. He started to sway, not so much a dance as what felt like a prelude to making love.

She melted against him and then grew tense when she felt his own desire stir and harden. She pulled away quickly.

"What do you think?" he asked.

What she thought was that she was in big trouble. Her expression must have given her away.

"What do you think about the floor?" he added quickly to clarify.

"It's spotless. I'm not sure it's ever been that clean before."

"Well, you've never had me before," Riley teased. "Now that you have, you'll want me back."

"I'm sure I can't afford you."

"I'm always willing to cut a deal."

And that she definitely couldn't afford. She finished her beer and got back to work while Riley went to find a ladder to get started on the ceiling fixtures and Tucker started setting up and cleaning the overturned tables and chairs.

Two hours later, Tucker slipped out to go pick up some tacos for lunch. Dani packed away the last unsalvageable gift item, some cup towels decorated with cupcakes. They were one of her best sellers, but she had another dozen or two in the storeroom.

Most of her money was made from bakery items, but the extras added to her bottom line.

The front doorbell rang again. Dani's muscles tensed. She wasn't afraid of Haggard with Riley and Tucker around, but if they got involved, the complications would increase.

She reached the door a step before Riley did. She took a deep breath and unlatched and opened the door. This time it was Angela Miles.

"I know I'm not supposed to come by for the interview until around four, but I heard about the burglary. I thought maybe there was something I could do to help you get the place cleaned up."

"How did you hear?"

"I was out at Hank's, you know, the country bar down the highway near the gravel pit."

"I know it." She'd never been there, but she'd heard of it.

"They have live music on Saturday and Sunday nights. Anyway, we dropped by there after the wedding. We were just having a beer and dancing when a couple of the deputies came in and started questioning some of the guys at the bar. Word gets around."

Apparently all the way out to Hank's.

"Did they arrest anyone yet?" Angela asked.

"Not that I've heard."

Since Angela was making no move to leave, Dani opened the door for her to come in.

"Oh, hi, Riley," Angela said. "I didn't know you were here."

"I forgot to post it on the town bulletin board," he said.

She laughed, a tinkling, flirtatious sound that didn't resemble anything that had ever come from Dani's mouth.

"I'm here to join the volunteers," Angela said. "Just tell me what to do, and I'll get busy. Maybe I can help you, Riley."

"I'm got my tasks covered. Dani gives the orders around here."

Dani considered Angela's offer, wondering what she was capable of doing, especially dressed the way she was. The red shorts came up to just below her navel and barely covered her rear. Her white blouse was tied above the waist, revealing a band of toned and tanned flesh. Her makeup was heavy, the mascara exceptionally thick for midday on Sunday.

"The display cabinet needs to be cleaned inside and out," Dani said. "Do you think you could handle that?"

"Do you have gloves? I just had my nails done."

"No gloves," she lied, wishing Angela would leave.

"Well, I'll just be careful," Angela said. "I can always get Eve at the Nail Spa to give me a touch-up."

Of course she could. Dani would guess Angela's hands had never been dirty and a broken nail would cause her extreme suffering.

Not only would hiring her be a big mistake, but just letting her in the door was also probably a big mistake.

But Angela had lost her son. Sometimes grief took a bizarre path to healing. Who was Dani to judge? Since Angela was here, Dani could at least give her a chance.

"Start with the outside of the display cases," Dani said.

"I don't want to get the front of my shirt wet. I'll just help Tucker," Angela said.

"No help needed," Tucker said.

She never started on the display cabinets, but merely flirted with the guys for a half hour and then had the nerve to ask about a job.

Dani reluctantly told her to show up at seven on Thursday and they'd see how things worked out.

If it went like today, she'd have no choice but to fire her before the busy weekend.

RILEY STOOD NEAR the front door, where he had a good look at the entire main room of the bakery. "Hard to believe this is the same place I walked into last night."

"And only a few dozen aching muscles later," Tucker added. "Did anyone take a 'before' picture? The transformation is amazing."

"I'd as soon never see that sight again, not even in a photograph," Dani said.

Riley stretched and straddled a chair. "Just too bad the guy who did the vandalizing wasn't the one to do the cleanup."

"With me standing over him with a whip," Tucker added.

"I'd have paid to watch that," Dani said.

"I bet it's one of your regulars," Tucker said, "or maybe one of your delivery people, like the FedEx guy, angry that you never offer him a warm cinnamon roll or a chocolate chip muffin."

Dani waved off the idea. "It's only the FedEx guy in extremely bad fiction, Sherlock. Besides, I always feed my deliverymen. The postman likes the raspberry scones and straight black coffee."

Tucker grinned. "I could go for one of those scones right now myself. But seriously, don't you have some idea who had motive to trash the place? Unjustified motive, but motive."

"No. And I'm sick of thinking about all this. Let it go."

There it was again, Riley thought. She was too quick to deny she suspected the identity of the culprit. Too determined not to discuss the possibilities.

She knew who'd wrecked her place, or at least

had a strong suspicion. But why not say—unless she was afraid of him?

He had to get to the bottom of this. To do that, he needed to get her alone—the sooner, the better.

Dani turned her back on both of them and walked toward the kitchen. "I'm going to wash my hands, start a pot of coffee and then go shower and change while the brew perks. I don't have any fresh raspberry scones, but I do have some of my special-recipe cowboy cookies to go with the coffee."

"And exactly what goes into those?" Riley asked.

"Chocolate chips, oatmeal, peanut butter, pecans and a secret ingredient."

"How secret?" Tucker asked.

"If I told you I'd have to ban you from my cookie jar forever."

He crossed his heart. "I swear I'll never ask again."

Riley leaned back, stretched his long legs out in front of him and cradled the back of his head in his hands. He studied Dani's movements, the way she held herself—she was natural, nothing fake or flaunting about her. Her hands were graceful as she attacked everything she did with easy precision.

He wondered how long it would take to reach the point where just the sight of her didn't stir a sensual desire.

"Infatuation becomes you," Tucker said, once Dani had gone upstairs.

"Am I that obvious?"

"Yep."

"It would be hard not to be turned on by Dani," Riley admitted. "She's like a sexy robot, never still, always focused on the task at hand. But then she's got this softness about her, too. She'd make a black bear want to cuddle."

"You do have a poetic side. Who knew?"

"Better than the X-rated limericks we used to make up as teenagers."

"I know. Some of those crazy things still come to mind from time to time. But back to Dani."

"Let's not. What I said probably doesn't make sense to you. I was never great at putting my feelings into words."

"No, I get what you mean about Dani. It's just I'm not sure she's being totally truthful with you or with any of us for that matter."

"Care to clarify?"

"She clammed up awful fast when I asked her about someone having motive to trash the bakery. It was clear she considered the subject off-limits."

"She did the same last night," Riley admitted. "I'm worried that someone may have it in for her. Hopefully, she'll trust me enough to level with me soon."

Tucker nodded. "Also, I have to wonder what she was thinking when she offered Angela Miles a job. That woman's a catastrophe waiting to happen. The way she was hanging on me a couple of times, I figured she should pay for us to get a room."

"Same here. Hell-bent on slutty, and I don't like saying that about any woman. I haven't had a chance to talk to Dani about her, but I figure she's sympathetic to the tragic and bizarre situation involving her father and the death of her son."

"Gotta say, that whole tragedy has the ring of a soap opera."

"I agree," Riley said. "Angela was a year behind me in school until we moved to Kansas to live with Uncle Raymond. She was always a spoiled brat. A form of affluenza, though we didn't have a name for it back then."

"And now her behavior is just weird. I know that Charlie thought the world of Dudley Miles, but now I have to think the whole Miles family is living on the edge of reason."

"I'm considering paying a visit to Dudley Miles."

"In prison?" Tucker asked.

"Why not? He's in a state facility not more than a couple of hours from here."

"I know he was charged with manslaughter, but how did that come about?" Tucker asked.

"The way Esther described it, he was supposed to be watching his toddler grandson, had a drink or two too many and the kid fell off the kitchen counter and died from a head injury.

"I won't bring up the reasons he's behind bars," Riley continued. "I'd just like to get his take on whether or not Charlie committed suicide."

"Good idea. Pierce may want to go with you. I

know he's still wrestling with that in his mind. I'd go, too, but I can't stay but a few more days and I think I'll do more good by helping out around the Double K."

"Yeah. I'll stick around until next week's roundup myself—maybe longer."

Maybe a lot longer, though if he was smart he'd run like crazy soon.

He knew himself. Too long in one place and the urge to roam would take over and he'd just wake up one day and hit the open road.

To the next ranch. The next adventure. Alone and uncomplicated.

It was his way.

RILEY LOWERED THE windows in his truck, letting the bracing air flow through Dani's hair and across her face. She was convinced that there was no more invigorating and beautiful time and place than April in the Texas Hill Country.

Trees and rolling pastures turned greener by the day and a million wildflowers burst into bloom with each new sunrise. The late afternoon sky was a background of royal blue, iced with layer upon layer of fluffy white clouds that looked as frothy as the whipped cream she doled out so generously in her shop.

Dani shifted in her seat so that she was facing Riley. He'd showered in her bathroom again before they left for the ranch. She had no doubt that for months to come she'd imagine him naked and glistening with suds every time she stepped into that same shower.

He smelled of soap and musk and a walk in the woods on a spring morning. He reeked of virility. And if she didn't stop thinking like this, she'd wind up in his arms again with or without any pretense of dancing.

She turned her gaze back to the road that stretched in front of them. The road Riley had come in on just yesterday on his way to the Double K Ranch.

The road he'd leave on any day now.

Riley reached over and flicked on the radio, keeping it low so that they could still talk if they had something to say. So far they'd ridden most of the way to the ranch in silence.

"Is the wind too much for you with the windows down?" he asked.

"No, it feels good. Clears the stench of bleach and cleansers out of my sinuses."

"I always ride with the windows down unless the heat and humidity are like an oven—which definitely happens when summer arrives full blast in Texas. Most women complain that it messes up their hair."

"Mine is always a mussed tangle of curls, so that's not a problem for me."

"I like your mussed look," he said. "It suits you."

"Mussed suits me? That doesn't sound exactly like a compliment."

"Ah, but it was. Makes me want to wind those curls around my fingertips. Makes you so touchable."

"Best not to while you're driving," she teased. "My curls are dangerous. Your fingers might become so entangled in the thick mass we'd end up in a wreck."

"Not if we pulled off onto the shoulder first or turned onto a dirt road."

She wasn't sure if he was serious or joking, but her insides quivered at the thought.

Her phone rang. Saved by the bell. She answered quickly, her voice tinged with the unfamiliar sensations rushing her senses. "Hello."

"Hi. It's Crystal. I just heard about the break-in. Are you and Constance okay?"

"We're fine." She explained the situation, providing only the details necessary for clarity.

"I hadn't heard about the vandalism. Is there anything I can do to help? Bring you dinner? Scrub floors? Come pick up Constance?"

"No. Constance spent last night at the Double K Ranch. I'm on my way to pick her up as we speak. The bakery is clean and ready to go."

"So you'll open again on Tuesday?"

"Believe it or not, I'm actually taking a few days off. I want to keep Constance having so much fun she can't worry about our being burglarized."

"I'm impressed and I think that's a great idea. I'm closed on Monday. Why don't we take the girls hiking at the state park? The drive there is beautiful this time of the year and we'll get some fresh air and exercise."

"I'd love to, but I have some business in San Antonio I have to take care of tomorrow."

"Then let Constance spend the day with us. The girls always have fun together."

That would be the perfect solution—provided the DNA kit actually arrived in the morning. Otherwise she'd have to take Constance into the city with her to be certain she collected the sample correctly.

"Constance would love a hiking outing, but can I get back to you in the morning? I want to get a feel for how Constance is handling all this first."

"Sure thing. And do let me know if I can do anything to help around the shop or if you just need a place to crash for a few days."

"I will, but right now everything's under control."

More specifically, as much under control as it could be under the circumstances.

By the time she'd broken the connection, Dani couldn't wait to see Constance. And once again she wondered what kind of perverted bastard James Haggard was that he basically wanted to sell his own daughter.

But then her sister had sold herself for far less than a million dollars, so this might be exactly the kind of man she'd have a child with.

Dani jumped from the truck the second Riley stopped in front of the sprawling ranch house. Constance met her at the door, all smiles and showing no sign of distress.

Dani pulled her into her arms and held so tight Constance pushed her away.

"You're hurting my ribs."

"Sorry, sweetheart. I missed you so much."

And she'd fight the devil himself to keep her safe. The scary part was, it might come down to exactly that.

## Chapter Nine

"Jaci couldn't ride the big Ferris wheel because she's too young, but I rode it with Carolyn Sawyer. Her little brother was too young to ride it, too."

Jaci put her hands on her hips. "I can ride it when I'm six."

"We both rode the carousel," Constance said, "and Esther rode it, too."

Esther put her right hand to her heart. "About the only kind of horse I can ride these days. That was enough excitement for me."

"I got prizes," Jaci said. "Want to see them?"

"Prizes? Wow," Dani said encouragingly. "Of course I want to see them."

"All I got was a whistle and some bubble-blowing liquid," Constance said, "but the bubble-blowing stuff is all gone. I shared with Jaci."

"That was nice."

For the past half hour or more, the girls had talked nonstop about their adventure at the spring carnival. Clearly, Constance hadn't let any concern about the break-in interfere with her fun. It was nice to be eight.

Jaci returned with her prizes, all five of them together probably worth less than a dollar. But she'd won them and that was all that mattered.

"You girls had positively too much fun," Riley said. "And yes, I'm talking about you, too, Esther."

Jaci and Constance giggled at the thought of Esther being a girl.

"I'm sorry I missed it," Dani said. "I can't thank you enough, Esther, for taking Constance with you."

"No trouble at all," Esther insisted.

"Keeping up with these two wound-up bundles of energy has to be exhausting. Constance and I will get out of here now and let you get some rest."

"You can't run off before supper," Esther said. "I'm making macaroni and cheese for the girls."

"That's far too much trouble."

"No, it isn't, Aunt Dani. Ple-e-ease. I love macaroni and cheese, and Tucker is fixing the rope on that broken tire swing so that Jaci and I can play on it."

"You've already put Tucker to work for you, too?"

"He'd promised Jaci yesterday that he'd get to it today," Esther said. "All my Lawrence boys are as good as their word. They got that from Charlie."

"We're not exactly boys anymore," Riley said, "but Charlie taught us a lot about good living and being a man of your word. That's no lie."

"C'mon, Jaci," Constance said. "Let's go see if the swing is fixed."

Dani gave up on the idea of leaving before supper. That wasn't a sacrifice on her part. Everything Esther cooked was delicious. Even better, the girls hadn't gotten tired and cranky and started fussing with each other yet.

In spite of the three years between them, they got along well most of the time. That was one of the reasons she and Grace had become such good friends so quickly. They were both new to town. They were both still learning to be caretakers of energetic, precocious little girls.

Grace's role as new stepmother was somewhat different than Dani's, but both Grace and Dani loved every part of their new lives, including the responsibility. Neither of them wanted to make a single mistake, though they knew that was impossible.

"Did you hear from Pierce or Grace today?" Dani asked.

"Heard from both of them," Esther said. "They were sipping margaritas on the River Walk and having a wonderful time."

"Sounds romantic," Riley said.

"Yes, but they're cutting the short honeymoon even shorter."

"Why?" Riley asked. "Is anything wrong?"

"Plenty." She reached over and patted Riley on the shoulder. "You and Tucker are here and Pierce is not. It's like we're having a family reunion without him."

"How does his new bride feel about that?"

"Land sakes. That wife of his is sweeter than stolen honey, and Grace understands Pierce. She's the one who made the decision that it was silly to be in San Antonio now when they can go there anytime."

"He's probably just worried Tucker and I aren't following all his orders," Riley joked.

"That, too," Esther agreed. "He told me to remind you to feed and water the horses tonight and Tucker to put out feed for the rest of the livestock and check on the pregnant cows."

"With all that to do around here, now I really feel terrible that I dragged you and Tucker off to help me," Dani said.

"Exactly," Riley agreed. "Now it's payback time. You get to help me take care of the horses."

"I'm not sure how much help I'll be. I know ridiculously little about horses."

"Not a problem. What you don't know, I'll teach you."

The humor in his tone and the mischievous glint in his eyes insinuated he wasn't only talking about horses. Fiery flashes of desire heated her senses.

They weren't strangers anymore. They'd spent most of the last two days together. In chaos, fun, frustration and cleansers.

It was inevitable that the sexual tension that tinged each touch, each moment they spent together, would eventually erupt into a roaring fire. That eruption might very well come tonight.

THIS WASN'T DANI'S first time in the Double K's horse barn, but it seemed entirely different this evening.

It seemed smaller, as if Riley sucked all the oxygen from the area and left her struggling for air. Every nerve in her body seemed to vibrate with anticipation, though she wasn't exactly sure what she was anticipating.

Wooden signs with the horses' names hung over each stall, but Dani was familiar enough with a few of them that she could recognize them even when they were in the pasture.

Some, like Dreamer and Beauty, she felt fairly comfortable around. The bigger stallions, like Rocket and Torpedo, she shied away from.

A few of the horses neighed as Riley walked past them on his way back to the feed storage area. Dreamer pawed and stuck her head over the top of her stall to be sure she was noticed. Beauty, the black quarter horse that Constance usually rode, pretended she didn't notice him.

Dani walked over to Beauty's stall and stood still for a few moments so as not to startle her. Then she put her hand out below the horse's nose, palms up, fingers pressed together, just as Pierce had shown her. Beauty lowered her head and stepped closer.

"Hello, Beauty. I don't usually get to visit you this late. Are you glad to see me?" She reached over the top of the stall and scratched the horse's neck and withers.

"I see you're not a total novice around horses," Riley said.

"Pierce, Grace and Esther have taken me under their wing."

"Have you fed the horses before?"

"Carrots, apple chunks or an occasional peppermint."

"Want to try ladling their grain mix into their feed pails? Unless you'd rather fill their water pails. The feed is easier."

He was serious about her helping. She felt foolish for thinking he had an ulterior motive for asking her to come with him. It was her own infatuation that was getting out of hand. "I'll feed them the grain if you show me how much and where to put it."

He gave her basic instructions and she measured the mixture and ladled it into the feed buckets as Riley took the pails to the outdoor hose and rinsed and refilled them.

He talked to the horses in a voice that calmed them and resulted in nuzzling and head movements that seemed to indicate they understood him. These were horses that had never seen him before yesterday.

He stopped at Huckleberry's stall. "What's the matter, boy? You've got a limp there. Want me to take a look at it?"

He opened the stall, squatted and picked up the right front hoof. "Looks like you have a stone wedged in there. Doesn't feel too good, does it? I'll take care of that. Won't even hurt."

Dani watched as he retrieved a hoof pick and loosened and removed the stone from the horse's hoof. Then he brushed the hoof thoroughly, removing smaller pieces of debris.

"We got it, boy. All done."

Huckleberry made a low nicking sound and nuzzled Riley's shoulder as if he was saying thank you. Dani stood silently and watched the show of affection, too moved to speak.

Finally she walked over to where Riley was putting away the brush. "Are you a horse whisperer?"

He laughed. "Never been called that before."

"But you're so good with the horses. It's like you're speaking the same language."

"Horses aren't that big a mystery if you pay attention to their actions. They show you what they need from you. Just like a man does. If you don't need the same, you have to let him know."

His voice had softened to a whisper. His gaze was intense, hypnotic, and she knew they were no longer talking about horses.

The need inside her swelled until she was dizzy.

Riley pulled her into his arms and lowered his face until their lips touched. In that moment every ounce of control vanished, melted in the heat of his kiss.

## Chapter Ten

Dizzy with desire, Dani swayed against Riley as the kiss deepened. The pulsing need swelled, vibrating through every erogenous cell in her body. She parted her lips, and his tongue slipped inside her mouth. Thrusting. Probing. Ravenous. As if he couldn't get enough of her.

He pulled her closer still and she arched toward him until his erection pressed hard against her trembling body. He lifted her and let her slide down the hard length of his need.

A soft moan escaped her lips and he slipped his right hand beneath her shirt, his fingers like fire on her skin as he traced a path to her breast. The first two snaps on her paisley Western shirt burst open.

He cupped her breasts and her nipples tingled and grew hard as he massaged and tweaked them. He sucked her bottom lip and then kissed his way down the smooth column of her neck until his face was buried in the swell of her breasts.

She couldn't think, couldn't deal with anything

except the pleasure that possessed her. Right or wrong, she was lost in the ecstasy with no will to fight it.

Her phone rang. She was so riveted to the carnal hunger that gripped her that she didn't even hear it until Riley pulled away. She checked the caller ID. "It's Cavazos."

"Damn bad timing that man has. But you should probably see what he wants."

She took a deep breath and exhaled slowly, hoping to regain enough composure that Cavazos didn't detect her passion overload over the phone. "Hello, Sheriff."

"Glad I caught you, Dani. I have good news. I think we've arrested your burglar. No proof yet, but my hunch is he's a credible suspect."

She hadn't expected that. "Who is it?"

"Young feller named Cory Boxer. He and a group of his fraternity brothers are using one of the fishing cabins a few miles up the river from here. Doing more partying than fishing from what I could tell."

His suspect was not James Haggard. There must be some mistake.

"Did Cory Boxer admit to the vandalism?"

"He's denying it, but one of my best deputies caught the guy red-handed, breaking in to the trunk of Joe Clark's car in broad daylight."

Joe Clark. She recognized the name. He and Jill owned the gift and card shop on Second Street, about two blocks from her bakery.

"Where was the car parked?" she asked.

"In the alleyway behind their shop. Joe carried in some boxes of merchandise he was helping Jill shelve. Wasn't in the shop more than a few minutes when he came out and saw Boxer standing over his open trunk and peering inside."

"Did Joe confront him?"

"He hollered at him. The guy took off running. Joe took off after him since he wasn't sure if he'd taken anything. One of my deputies spotted them and he stepped in and made the arrest."

"But he denied breaking in to my shop?"

"Yes, but he also argued he wasn't up to no good when Joe saw him with his head stuck in the trunk."

"Was anything missing from the trunk?"

"Nope. Luckily, Joe spotted him before he made off with his laptop which was right there in plain sight. Darn shame when a man has to lock his car downtown in broad daylight."

Still, checking out an unlocked truck in a deserted alley wasn't quite the same as breaking into and vandalizing a bakery.

"We'll get a fingerprint check to make sure we have the right guy, but just wanted you to know you can rest easier tonight. I've got a prime suspect in central lockup for twenty-four hours."

"I appreciate your calling."

A stranger with no motive to wreck her business. If the sheriff was right, the DNA she'd collected was worthless to her. She was back to square one again. Except... "Did Cory Boxer have any wounds?"

"Matter of fact, he had some ugly scratches on one arm. Said a cat got hold of him. Why do you ask?"

"I found some blood. I think my vandal must have hurt himself in the process."

"Makes more sense than getting scratched by a cat. I reckon you've seen the last of this kind of trouble, hopefully for a good long while."

"Yes, hopefully," she agreed. But even if Cory Boxer had broken into her shop, this was not the last of James Haggard.

When the call was finished, she shared the news with Riley.

"You don't sound very relieved," he said.

Surprisingly, she wanted to spill the full truth to him. The anxiety had burgeoned with the sheriff's arrest of a suspect other than Haggard. Or maybe she just wanted some reassurance that she was making the right decisions.

It was too chancy to drag him into this while she was still reeling from his kisses.

He'd go his way in a few days. If it turned out Haggard was Constance's biological father, her battles would be just beginning.

THE GLOW OF twilight painted the sky with wide brushes of burnished gold. It was the time of day on a ranch when the magic came together—the time Riley felt like the luckiest man on earth, living the dream.

A lot of cowboys he knew were poets. He'd always wished words came that easy to him, but mostly he just responded with a peaceful feeling, at home with himself and the whole beautiful country to roam.

Tonight held a different kind of magic that had nothing to do with the pastoral splendor. It had everything to do with Dani Boatman.

He couldn't explain it, no more than he could explain the lure of the open range. He couldn't deny it, either. He felt things differently with Dani.

It wasn't just the way she'd turned him on back in the horse barn. He'd felt that way even before they'd kissed. He couldn't imagine ever getting enough of her. This was not how his visit to Texas was supposed to go.

He'd figured he'd visit with his brothers and Esther, get acquainted with his niece and new sister-in-law, do some fishing and then head out to West Texas before all that togetherness started to make him feel fenced in.

No reflection on his brothers or Esther, but it was Dani he wanted to be with. Mostly it was just enjoying her company, but the need to protect her was high on the list, too. And that was where he found himself now.

The facts didn't add up. Dani should have been relieved that the sheriff had arrested a suspect. Instead, she'd seemed annoyed or worried. Also, she'd never mentioned finding bloodstains to him, though he must have been nearby when she discovered them.

There was more going on than she was admitting. Somehow he had to find a way to get her to open up to him.

The front door opened and Dani and Constance stepped out, joining him on the porch. Constance was dragging her backpack, the head of a freckled doll in braids that looked a lot like her peeking out of the half-zipped bag.

Dani had her handbag over her shoulder and a reusable green bag no doubt filled with eggs or something from Esther's garden.

"I was wondering where you'd gotten off to," Dani said. "I was looking for you to tell you goodbye."

"It's early. With all the talk and laughter surrounding that board game you were playing, I didn't expect you to be leaving for hours."

"I wasn't ready to go," Constance assured him. "Aunt Dani said we have to."

"I'm the baddie," Dani joked. "If only we didn't need sleep."

"Oh, wait," Constance called, forgetting her argument. "I left my whistle." She went rushing back into the house.

Dani laughed. "I should have tossed that squeaky toy while I had the chance."

She started down the steps. Riley walked beside her, hesitant to see her leave without him.

He couldn't get past the uneasiness she'd exhibited when taking to the sheriff. Nor could he brush off the impression she'd given last night and again today that she knew or at least strongly suspected the identity of the intruder.

"I think you should invite me home with you for a slumber party," he said, trying for a nonchalance he didn't feel.

"Sounds tempting, I admit, but I'm not ready to go there with Constance in the house."

"I'll sleep on the sofa and I promise I won't make a move on you tonight, even if you beg," he teased.

"Such a gentleman. I don't think you'd even fit on my sofa." She stopped by her car and looked up at him. "What's this really about, Riley?"

"I think you might be uneasy staying alone so soon after the break-in."

"I'll be fine. Seriously. You secured the back door. You can't be my full-time caretaker."

"Just until you get the alarm system fixed."

"I'll call them first thing in the morning. The sheriff indicated I have nothing to worry about."

But he wasn't sure she believed Cavazos, and if she didn't, how could he?

"If you don't share your sofa, I'll camp out on the street in front of the bakery," he said. "Imagine the gossip that will cause."

"Do you ever take no for an answer, Riley Lawrence?"

"All depends on the question."

She rolled her eyes. "Okay, but follow me back in your truck. I'll need my car in the morning."

"Give me a minute to grab a few necessities like a razor and a toothbrush."

She'd given in too easily, which meant she was somewhat nervous about her and Constance being alone tonight even if she wasn't admitting that to him. She might not even be admitting it to herself.

The next challenge was finding a way to make her trust him enough to tell him the truth about what was going on. Which meant he'd have to keep his word not to come on to her tonight.

And that might take all the control he could muster.

JAMES HAGGARD HEARD the blaring sounds of a mediocre country band when he stepped out of his pickup truck in Hank's parking lot. He wouldn't stay long. Two beers at the most. It was when he was drunk or high that he made foolish mistakes.

Like breaking in to Dani's Delights.

His brother, Lenny, had warned him to stay in the cabin and make sure he wasn't seen around town until he went back to pick up his money on Friday.

Lenny was always right. He took care of James. Always had. He was the only who'd never lied to James, or cheated him. The only one who didn't take advantage of him every chance he got. The only one James trusted.

But Lenny wasn't the one stuck inside that cheap, ratty cabin that stank like dead fish. He had to get out for a little while or he'd go crazy. He walked through the double doors into the stench of stale smoke and the tantalizing smell of whiskey. He went straight to the bar and dropped onto a tall stool.

"A shot of Jack. Make that a double," he added, already backing down from his vow of sticking to two beers. He gulped down the whiskey in one swallow and swiveled so that he could see the band.

The female singer reminded him of Amber back in the day, except that the singer wasn't nearly the looker Amber had been. In his mind, he always remembered her as she'd looked the night they'd met. Short white shorts, a halter top, no bra and those bright red stiletto heels.

Her auburn hair cascaded down her back in loose curls. And those lips, those full, heart-shaped lips that could drive any man crazy.

But she'd changed. She'd treated him like dirt. Walked all over him. He motioned to the bartender. "Another double."

The singer might not be as pretty as Amber, but he'd bet she was the same two-timing, double-crossing, bitch Amber had become. And after all he'd done for her.

He was Constance's father. Half of that damn insurance money rightly belonged to him. Dani had better believe he meant business.

A blonde strutted over and took the stool next to him. "Want to buy a girl a drink?"

"Sure." He looked her over. Firecracker-hot. A red dress that hugged every curve. A little drunk, but he might be there himself in a few minutes. "You got a name?"

"Angela." She leaned in close, giving him a good look at the breasts pushing out of a scrap of lacy black bra. "I haven't seen you around here before."

"Just passing through."

"Too bad. We might have gotten to know each other."

He put a hand on her thigh. She didn't move it away.

"We can still get to know each other," he ventured. "We just have to work faster."

She laughed, a tinkling sound that crawled right under his skin.

The night might not be such a drag after all.

RILEY QUICKLY CAUGHT up with Dani's car. He followed it to the downtown area but pulled away at the head of Main Street. Driving slowly, he took the alley that ran behind her shop.

The area was quiet without even a cat to be seen tonight. The bakery's back door was still boarded over just as he and Tucker had left it last night. He stopped, crawled from beneath the wheel and took the few steps to the fenced area.

All clear, so he turned at the corner and drove back to Main Street. Ten before nine on a Sunday night and the locals were settled in for the night. The quiet isolation, the hitching posts, the century-old wooden buildings and the soft glow from the antique streetlights gave the eerie impression that he'd stepped into the Old West.

He pulled into the diagonal parking spot next to Dani's car. She was standing at the open back door. He didn't see Constance until he was standing next to Dani.

"She's sound asleep," Dani whispered. "Has been almost ever since we left the ranch. Little stinker would never have admitted that she was tired."

Dani tugged on Constance's arm. "Wake up, baby. We're home."

Constance mumbled in her sleep and curled even tighter into the fetal position.

"We're home, sweetheart. You have to get out of the car so we can go inside."

Constance opened her eyes and rubbed them with her fists. Dani helped her to a sitting position and managed to get her to the edge of the seat.

"Let her sleep," Riley said. "I'll tote her upstairs. What's the use of having your own cowboy body-guard if you can't get a few perks?"

Riley reached down and picked her up, carrying her as if she was an oversize doll. "You get the door," he said. "I'll carry her up to her bed."

Constance's arms tightened around his neck and she rested her head on his shoulder. His throat grew dry, making it difficult to swallow. He wasn't sure he'd ever carried a kid before. The most he'd done was help one in or out of a saddle. This felt too...

He wasn't sure what it felt. Too much like a family? Too involved? Too fatherly.

He experienced a sudden suffocating sensation. What the hell was a man like him doing in a situation like this? His breathing came hard as he pushed back the impulse to get back in his truck and drive away.

Instead he started walking calmly toward the bakery as the frightening truth hit full force. He was already where he really wanted to be.

DANI GULPED IN a deep breath as she stepped into her bakery and let the familiarity seep into her bones. The lingering odors of spices and baking bread. The empty display cases calling out to be filled. The chairs and tables awaiting customers.

For a man like Riley, who never settled in one place long enough to put down roots, this life probably felt like fatal boredom. To her, it was a dream come true.

Their lives would never mesh. They were a few days in a lifetime, a thrill that would live in her memories, a mountain high before the next valley. As long as she didn't expect more than that, she'd be fine.

She set Constance's backpack on the floor and went back to the car for the two dozen fresh eggs Esther had insisted she bring home with her. She checked to make sure Riley's car was locked and then opened the passenger-side door of her car to retrieve the eggs.

She sniffed and caught the stench of cigarette smoke and alcohol. Footfalls approached from the street behind her. She jumped back from the car as panic rocked her ragged nerves.

"Luch who sh-h-owed up."

Dani's heart flew to her throat. Even with the drunken slur, there was no mistaking James Haggard's voice.

## Chapter Eleven

Haggard staggered forward and fell against Dani's front bumper.

"You're drunk," she said.

"Damn r-r-right." He stumbled nearer.

She scanned the area. Only two cars other than hers were parked on this block. Both of them belonged to shop owners with upstairs living quarters. "How did you get here?"

Haggard waved his arm as if dismissing her question. His hand was bandaged. She stared at it, breathing hard. It was his blood she'd collected. *His* DNA. Her instincts screamed that was true, but she needed proof.

"Why did you break in to my shop last night?" she demanded. "What were you looking for?"

His response was a string of profanity and words so slurred she couldn't make sense of them.

"You were here last night," she persisted. "Admit it."

He mumbled a curse and then used the cuff of his shirt to wipe spittle from his lips and chin.

"I'm not afraid of you, James Haggard. Wrecking my shop won't help you get what you want."

"Wre-e-ecked it. Next time. Burn it down."

The slurred pronouncements were followed by another assault of foul language.

But he had said next time, which had to mean he'd been here last night. The blood she'd collected was his. That was all she needed to know.

Dani tried to push past him. Haggard grabbed her right arm. He lost his balance and fell against her, clutching her shirt with both hands in an effort not to slam to the pavement.

Miraculously, she managed to hold both of them up.

"What the devil…"

Dani looked up as Riley flew out the door and stormed across the walk. Reaching down, he grabbed Haggard by his shirt collar and yanked him away from Dani.

She grabbed Riley's right arm as he was about to punch Haggard. "Don't. He's just drunk. I know him."

Haggard tried to shove Riley away. Riley easily pinned him against the car.

"Your friend needs to learn some manners," Riley said.

"I said I know him. I didn't say he was a friend."

Haggard started cursing again, spraying the air with saliva. Riley let go of him and Haggard slid slowly down the fender, landing on his butt, his shoulder pressed against the tire.

"Call 911," Riley said. "He can sleep it off in jail."

And then the law would be involved and things might spin out of control just as Haggard had warned. A custody suit. Constance used as a pawn.

"I'd rather not bring the law into this."

"I seem to be missing something here. Exactly how well do you know this man?" Riley asked.

"Not well," she admitted.

"If you know where he lives, I'll drive him home."

"I don't."

"What about the name of someone in his family we can call to come get him?"

She shook her head. "I don't know anything about him. He's just a customer."

"Then what's your problem with letting law enforcement handle this, especially considering someone broke into and vandalized your bakery last night?"

She hated lying to Riley and knew it was unlikely that he was buying her story. No one would. But if she gave Riley any part of the truth, he'd manage to get the whole story out of her.

He'd jump into the middle of the situation.

Subconsciously, she might even want that, but it wouldn't be fair to Riley on any level and she might completely lose control of everything.

Dani watched as Riley helped Haggard to a standing position and then half dragged the intoxicated man to the metal bench across the street from the bakery. Haggard's feet stretched out in front of him. He slumped forward. His eyes closed.

Riley walked back to Dani and took her hands in his. "Here's the deal. We're going inside and you're going to tell me the truth. The actual truth and not some doctored version of the facts. Once I know what the hell is going on, we'll decide what to do with your vulgar-mouthed, drunk acquaintance."

"You'd be wiser to get in your truck and drive away."

"Probably, but I've got a mighty strong hunch that you're in a heap of trouble, Dani Boatman, and like it or not, you need my help."

He was right, of course. Things had gone too far, become incredibly complicated. Continuing the lies wouldn't be fair to him.

Once they were back inside, she searched for a truthful way of presenting the details that didn't scream for his help. Riley listened to Dani's bizarre explanation and to his credit he didn't interrupt or comment until she'd finished.

He stared incredulously. "What kind of fool would expect you to just turn over a million dollars without any proof to back up his claims of paternity?"

"The kind of fool you just helped to the bench. Only he talked as if I already knew he was the father and deliberately cut him out of money that was rightfully his."

"How were you supposed to have gotten that information?"

"From Constance's original birth certificate."

"Where is her birth certificate?"

"Upstairs in my safe. No father is listed. I told him that, but I don't think he believed me."

"Sounds like he's a practiced rip-off artist to me," Riley said. "He may not even know your sister or Constance. He might have heard or read about the insurance settlement and is trying to con you out of the cash."

"I wouldn't put that past him," she agreed. "But I can't know that for sure without seeing DNA test results."

"If he is Constance's biological father and thought he had a chance in hell of getting custody, he wouldn't bother with you," Riley said. "He'd file for custody and try to cash in on the entire settlement."

"He admitted he doesn't want custody. He wants cash—by Friday at noon."

"I'm sure he does. You surely aren't planning to give it to him."

"I couldn't even if I wanted to. The money is in a trust fund for Constance and can't be touched until she's twenty-one. The one exception is that she can draw out an allowance to pay for college and living expenses if she is a full-time student at the accredited university of her choice."

"Did you tell Haggard that?"

"All except the college stipulation. He didn't believe me or else he thinks there is some way around that. He wants his money within the week or he files for custody."

"Nothing but trash talk from a con man and that's the best I can say about him. I should have punched the drunken thug when I had the chance."

Physical violence was the last thing she needed.

"Call the sheriff, Dani. Tell him exactly what you just told me. He won't even have to go looking for Haggard to arrest him."

"It's not that simple."

"It is the way I see it. Get a restraining order to keep the lunatic away from you and Constance. If Haggard still gives you trouble, the Lawrence brothers will pay him a visit. We can be very persuasive."

"I'm sure you can, but I can't take chances with Constance's future. I have to do this my way."

"What is your way?"

Dani explained the blood sample she'd collected and the paternity-test kit that should arrive in the morning. "With luck, I'll have the test results back by Thursday or Friday. If they show Haggard is not Constance's father, I'll call the sheriff and press charges immediately."

"And if he is?"

"I'll do whatever it takes to make sure he never gets custody."

"In that case I'm going with you to San Antonio in the morning."

She threw her hands up in exasperation. "I can handle this. They need you at the ranch."

"Tucker will be there and Pierce is heading back in the morning."

"He's cutting his honeymoon short so that he can spend time with you and Tucker."

"My brothers would do the same in these circumstances. Besides, I will be spending time with them and so will you and Constance. There's no reason your ranch vacation can't start tomorrow night."

"I can't believe you'd still want me there."

"I've always been a sucker for a woman who looks good in jeans and can bake croissants. I do have one question, though."

"I was afraid you might."

"You collected the blood last night. You must have strongly suspected then that Haggard was behind the break-in. Why didn't you admit that to me?"

"I didn't want to drag you into my problems."

He walked over, caught her wrist and pulled her into his arms. "Is that the only reason?"

"No. I didn't trust you to understand. I barely knew you, Riley. We had no basis of trust."

He nudged her chin with his thumb until she met his gaze. "Do you trust me now?"

"I'm trying, Riley. It's just so hard to let go. I've never had anyone to depend on but myself."

"Now you do. I can't explain what's going on between us, Dani. I do know that if you don't let me protect you I'll go crazy. How's that for my scientific analysis?"

He kissed her on the tip of her nose and then let his lips brush hers. The need swelled inside her, but he pulled away.

"Go upstairs and get some rest," he whispered. "Just toss a sheet and a pillow on the sofa. I'll be up later."

"I should check on Haggard first—see if he's sober enough to say where he's staying. I may need that information for future reference."

"I'll check on the swindler."

"Okay." She turned and started toward the stairs. She stopped on the bottom step. "Riley."

"What is it?"

"You really shouldn't be here, but thanks. See you at breakfast."

Breakfast with Dani. Crazy how much he liked the sound of that.

RILEY WAITED UNTIL Dani reached the top of the stairs and then walked into her gleaming kitchen. There wasn't much in there he dared to touch, but he had watched her make coffee in the small French press that morning and he felt good about tackling that.

Probably easier than brewing a pot over an open campfire, though it wouldn't give the same level of satisfaction—especially since he was making this pot for Haggard. He couldn't care less if the jerk slept on the bench all night or curled up under it.

His concern was getting the point across to Haggard that the man's underhanded, thieving gig was up. Keep messing with Dani and he'd answer to Riley. Riley never started a fight without good cause, but he never backed down from one that needed to be won.

He filled a tall white mug with the brew and took it outside to try to rouse Haggard. A brisk breeze carried the fragrance of honeysuckle and jasmine from a hanging pot across the street.

All was quiet. Too quiet. No guttural snoring. No ragged breathing.

The bench was empty.

Either someone had picked Haggard up, or that was the fastest damn sobering up Riley had ever seen. He flicked on his phone's flashlight app and checked the space between their parked vehicles to make sure he hadn't staggered there. No luck.

He walked back and shot beams of light around and beneath the bench to see if Haggard had dropped anything that might give a clue to where he was staying. There was nothing.

A deputy or town constable patrolling the area could have picked him up, but if so, it was odd Riley hadn't noticed any flashing blue lights through the bakery's large window.

Which meant there was a good chance Haggard was not in this alone. So, was it his blood Dani had collected or that of an accomplice? Would the test she was putting so much faith in prove nothing at all?

BREAKFAST IN THE small kitchen of the cozy second-floor living space was mistake one of the new day. An emotional wreck from the chaotic weekend and her unexpected infatuation with Riley, Dani needed a break from the nonstop sensual overload.

She wasn't getting it. Riley had insisted on "fixin' up" an authentic Texas, trail-ride breakfast even though it meant a quick trip to the local market for fresh tortillas and ingredients for fresh-made *pico de gallo.*

He wanted to prove he wasn't completely without skills in the kitchen, he'd said.

She hadn't needed that proof. She'd experienced his kitchen skills Friday night and was still re-covering. Sleeping a room away from him last night hadn't helped the recuperative process.

And now this.

The food was not the mistake. The problem was the three of them gathered around the comfy din-ing nook talking, laughing and passing around the *pico de gallo* and extra grated cheese as if they were a family.

Not the kind of family setting Dani had ever known and probably not Constance, either. She wasn't sure about Riley's family life, except that his parents were killed when he was fourteen and he and his brothers had come to live with Charlie and Esther Kavanaugh.

She did know he was a rambler, which made their relationship and this easy familiarity all the more confusing. He was determined to protect her, but what did he really want in return?

And the most puzzling aspect of all—why Dani? If he was looking for a fast and easy fling, why not go for a thin, sexy, fun-and-games hottie like Angela Miles instead of a plump pastry chef whose life was a boiling pot of trouble?

She took a bite of her fried egg and sausage taco. The combination of flavors exploded in her mouth.

"And the verdict?" Riley asked.

"Great, but with a kick."

He leaned over—close—as if he was about to kiss her. At the last second, he dabbed the corner of her mouth with a napkin. "You may have overdone it with the salsa."

Her pulse slowed to near normal, but the air was thick with sensual tension.

"I like tortillas, but not as much as I like Aunt Dani's cinnamon rolls," Constance said, breaking the tension without even knowing it existed.

"Yes, but could she make cinnamon rolls out on the trail over a campfire?"

"No, I can't, cowboy, and I have no intention to try it."

"Is this really what cowboys eat on the trail?" Constance asked.

"It is if you're in Texas and lots of other places. The vaqueros have been a major influence in the ranching world."

"What's a vaquero?"

"That's Spanish for cowboy."

"Have you ever been on a cattle drive?"

"Yep. Many times. I don't usually do the cooking, though."

"What do you do?"

"Keep the cattle moving in the right direction."

"Or they might get lost?"

"A good cowboy will never let that happen."

"I wish I could go on a cattle drive."

"You'd have to miss too much school for that, but maybe we should start getting in shape for that tomorrow with a sunrise trail ride out at the Double K Ranch. I hear you're a good rider."

"I am. Jaci's daddy taught me. Can I go, Aunt Dani? Puh-leeeze." She put her hands together in prayer formation.

Dani realized she'd been had. Riley had just made it practically impossible now to back out of spending at least one day at the ranch. Not that she wanted to back out, but who knew what complication James Haggard would hurl her way next?

"Please, Aunt Dani?" Constance begged again. "There's no school and I finished my homework, even the word problems."

"Reneging is a coward's way out," Riley said.

Dani gave up. Saying no to Constance's pleadings and Riley's insistence would amount to cruel and unusual punishment—mostly to Dani.

"A trail ride sounds fun," she said, relenting. "As long as I can come along."

"The more the merrier," Riley said.

Riley reached for a second soft breakfast taco.

Constance took a second bite of her first one.

The shop's doorbell rang.

"I'll get it," Riley said.

"No, let me," Dani insisted. She dashed to the landing and then down the stairs, aware that Riley was right behind her.

*Please let it be the overnight delivery of the DNA kit and not James Haggard coming back to finish what he'd started before he vanished in the night.*

# Chapter Twelve

A FedEx truck stopped in the middle of the street, blocking Lenny Haggard's view of the front door of Dani's Delights. Package in hand, the delivery-man got out, walked between a pickup truck and Dani Boatman's car and approached the bakery's front door.

Lenny Haggard folded the newspaper he'd been pretending to read, got up from the bench where he'd found his irresponsible, screw-up of a brother last night and crossed the street for a better view.

The printed sign on the shop's front door read Closed until Thursday, but he knew Dani was on the premises. He'd spotted movement upstairs through the open windows. That didn't mean she wasn't about to take Constance and go on the run rather than hand over money that she knew wasn't rightfully hers.

The door to the bakery opened and Dani stepped outside. She looked as if she was dressed to travel. Nice slacks, a white blouse with a bright green cardigan. A minimum of makeup, but she looked damn good.

Not a stunner like Amber had been at her peak, but then he'd met only a handful of women in his life who could measure up to Amber's beauty and sparkle when she'd first dropped into his life.

DANI SIGNED FOR DELIVERY. The package was about the size of a shoe box, so not the right shape for legal documents that might indicate she was moving money around—for good or bad.

When the deliveryman turned to leave, Lenny rushed toward Dani. His ignorant brother had done nothing but mess things up. Lenny would handle this from here on out, the way he should have all along.

A few steps before he reached the opposite curb, a tall, muscled guy appeared at the door and joined Dani. Lenny turned away and kept walking. His plan would work much better if he caught her alone.

She was getting a reprieve this morning, but this was far from over. All he had to do was convince Dani Boatman that he wasn't playing around. He had to have that money. He had to have it fast or all he had to look forward to was three holes in the back of his brain.

He wouldn't go down alone.

IT WAS EXACTLY 1:16 p.m. when Dani and Riley stepped out of the Corinthian Court Lab and into bright sunshine and a cool spring breeze. She felt lighter than she had at any time since James Haggard appeared in her life like a venomous snake, spewing his poison into every corner of her existence.

"We're just a few blocks from the River Walk," Riley said. "How about we head there and find a restaurant along the waterway?"

"A great idea. All of a sudden I'm starved."

"You should be, since you only ate a few bites of my mouthwatering breakfast."

"Sorry. I promise it wasn't your cooking. It's just that my stomach was in knots."

"And now it's not?"

"Surprisingly, no. Temporarily, at least. It helps that I've finally done something proactive instead of just waiting for Haggard to hit with his next attack."

"I still think we should tell Cavazos and hand the case over to him," Riley said.

"I know, but I'd really like to know if James is Constance's biological father first. You've almost convinced me of one thing, though. I've thought a lot about something you said last night."

"I'm thrilled to get an honorable mention. What gem of my wisdom weighed in?"

"That if James Haggard was certain he could prove he was Constance's father, he'd have gone directly to the courts with that information and tried to weasel his way into getting all the money."

"That's definitely how I see it," Riley agreed. "Whereas if his name is on the birth certificate, all he has to do is convince you the information is accurate in hopes you'll be so worried about losing Constance or the money you'll play right into his hands."

"Which means he believes his name is on the certificate, but he's not sure she's his child. It hurts to say this, but knowing my sister the way I do, I think there's a good chance she didn't even know whose sperm impregnated her."

"So unless the paternity test comes out positive for Haggard, you still won't know the identity of Constance's father."

"So an endless chain of men could show up claiming to be her father. Thank you, Riley Lawrence, for returning the knots to my stomach."

"A good prickly pear margarita will fix that."

"It may take two."

Riley took her arm as they crossed the street and continued to the concrete steps that descended to the network of beautiful arched bridges and walkways that ran along both sides of the San Antonio River.

The streets were lined with shops, restaurants and colorful umbrellas and decorations that celebrated the Mexican heritage so closely connected with San Antonio. A brightly decorated barge filled with people cruised the shallow waterway.

Dani raced down the remaining few steps and then crossed the first bridge she came to, stopping at the top of the arch for a better view of the lively waterway. "It's beautiful. Are you sure we're still in the same country?"

"Don't tell me this is your first visit to San Antonio?"

"No. I drove to the city several times when I was getting the bakery up and running, but all the supply shops were on the outskirts of town. There was never any time to spare, since I had to hurry back before Constance got home from school."

"You and Constance have got to get out more."

"We are. We're about to visit what I hear is a very exciting ranch."

"It will be, once you arrive."

"Problems and all?"

"You just left those behind at a highly rated lab. The next few days are fun, relaxation and getting to know each other better. Much better."

He reached for her hand and squeezed it, leaving no doubt what he meant. Hot pangs of anticipation stirred a new wave of desire. She wanted to taste his lips, wanted to explore the passion he ignited with his touch.

Wanted to escape her own inhibitions and go where temptation led her.

But could she do that knowing this had nowhere to go, knowing she'd be just another charm to add to his collection?

"We'll have to come back during the Christmas season," Riley said, "when the entire River Walk glistens from the illumination of millions of tiny lights. Then it really does look magical."

"And which Christmas are you likely to make it back to Texas for, Riley Lawrence?"

He hesitated, then shrugged. "Guess I'd have to figure that one out."

In other words, don't count on him. No surprise. She'd known that from the beginning. But he was here today and she needed this fairyland break from reality. "Where do we go for those margaritas you were touting?"

"We're almost there."

RILEY SIPPED HIS MARGARITA, his gaze fastened on Dani as she dipped her chip into a bowl of guacamole. When she parted her lips and slipped the chip into her mouth, desire bucked deep inside him. Nothing about this crazy attraction made sense. He'd been with lots of women. Some prettier than Dani. Some younger. Some older. Some with kids—some without.

None had ever intrigued him the way Dani did. He liked her verve, her spark and determination, the way she took on life. He'd seen it that first morning when she just kept pouring coffee, serving pastries and smiling as the line snaked around the room. She'd been flustered but still congenial, and greeted every customer in a way that made them forgive her for the wait.

He was impressed by her business savvy, her cooking skills and her relationship with Constance.

A lot of young, single women would have resented having to take over the care of a motherless niece. Dani acted like it was a gift from the gods. James Haggard might not know it yet, but even without Riley's intervention, he had met his match.

Not that Riley was going anywhere until Haggard was gone for good.

Dani picked up the lunch menu and studied it. "It all looks wonderful. Any suggestions?"

"I've had their chicken enchiladas verdes before. They're great. If you like lobster, the lobster empanada is excellent. All their tostados are good. Or we could share fajitas if you're up for that. You might want to bear in mind that while suppers at the ranch are usually light, Esther can't resist an overflowing table when she has a full house."

"Are you certain you checked this ranch vacation out with Esther and that she's good with it?"

"How well do you know Esther?" he teased.

Dani laughed. "You're right. You could invite half the town over and she'd just start smiling and frying chicken. She's ecstatic over having her three *boys* home, as she refers to you and your brothers."

"If she's still around when we go on Medicare, we'll still be her boys."

"And here I am, stealing you away again."

"And you had to work so hard at it."

The waitress came by to take their order.

"If you need a few more minutes, that's fine," she assured them.

"I think we're ready." Dani turned back to him. "Are you still in for sharing fajitas?"

"I'm in. The combo fajitas for two, with extra jalapenos."

"Will there be anything else?" the waitress asked.

"Not for me," Dani said.

"That'll do it," he agreed.

Dani commented on the sightseeing barges on the waterway and the pedestrians strolling by a few steps from their table. Bringing her here was a great idea. She needed this taste of normalcy in her life.

Keeping her mind off James Haggard until she heard the results would be a challenge.

She turned back to face him. "You're a hard man to figure, Cowboy Riley."

"Only if you're looking for something hidden beneath the surface. I am what you see. No surprises or great depths to be discovered."

"I don't believe that. What was your life like growing up in Winding Creek?"

"That's going back a long way."

"Not that long. You're, like, what? Twenty-five?"

"Twenty-eight. You?"

"Twenty-six. That gets the basics out of the way. So back to your life growing up as the middle brother."

"The typical life. We lived in town. Went to local schools. Never worried about much except getting in trouble for not doing our homework or for breaking something while wrestling inside the house."

Odd, but he didn't think about that life much anymore. It was like his pre-life, before the tragedy that had reshaped the rest of his life.

"A good life," Dani said. "The kind I hope to give Constance from here on out."

He nodded. "A good life. Safe. I guess if I had to describe those years in one word, it would be safe."

He'd never thought of it that way before, and he seldom dwelled on that part of his past, but it was true.

"And then my parents left one morning and never came back. They were there and then they were gone. Killed in a five-vehicle pileup on the way to San Antonio."

"How traumatic to lose both your parents at once. How old were you then?"

"Fourteen. I was angry with them at first." He'd never told anyone that before, wasn't sure he'd ever admitted that to himself. The truth had always had a way of hiding inside him, tamped down so tightly it couldn't escape.

Dani had somehow loosened the cap, releasing even the darkest of memories.

"I remember one day standing on the edge of the gorge at Lonesome Branch. I came within inches of ending my life that day. Instead, I stood there and screamed curses at my parents for leaving me until I finally broke into sobs."

"Anger is a natural step in dealing with grief."

"I wasn't reasoning all that out at the time."

"I'm sure. A trauma like that would knock you off-kilter at any age."

"Yep. Thankfully Charlie Kavanaugh taught me the value of climbing back into the saddle even when you think you don't have the courage to try."

"And he obviously got you hooked on the cowboy lifestyle."

"I owe him big for that." Owed him enough he should be digging a lot deeper into whether or not Charlie's death was actually a suicide.

"It may seem odd, but in the days that followed, the gorge became my special place to go when something good or bad happened in my life. The spot where I went to celebrate or just to get my head on straight."

"Everyone needs a place like that."

"Where is yours?"

"I guess I'd have to say it's in my kitchen making dough."

"I get that. I hate to change the subject, but would you mind if we make a quick stop at the prison on our way back to Winding Creek? It's only a few miles out of the way."

"For you to see Dudley Miles?"

"Yeah. How did you guess?"

"I've heard Esther talk about what great friends Charlie and Dudley were."

"And had been for years. Good men. Strong

willed, but fair and honest. Both had ranching in their blood. Seems unreal that their lives would take such bizarre and disastrous twists within months of each other."

"I know. That's why I gave in to Angela's mother's pleas that I give Angela a job. To lose a child and have your father go to prison for manslaughter and then hide the evidence by trying to get rid of the body must be taking its toll on her."

"Your decision, but don't be surprised if it doesn't work out with Angela. My guess is she's got more problems than a job can fix."

"I'm afraid I agree, and, of course, I don't mind stopping off at the prison. Why don't you give them a call while I take a restroom break and see what you can arrange?"

Riley watched her walk away. Damn, did she look good leaving! Almost as good as she did coming. And that was with her clothes on. His body sprang to life just imagining what she'd look like with them off.

He motioned to their waitress. "One more margarita for the lady."

"And for yourself?"

"Designated driver. I'll take a sweet iced tea."

He looked up the phone number for the prison and made the call. After a few runarounds to different departments and several on-holds, the visit was arranged.

He wasn't sure how to approach Dudley or what

he expected to get out of him that might help. He just felt like he owed this to Charlie.

DANI STROLLED THE aisles of dozens of open-air stalls that dotted Greenhorn Fairgrounds. Spring Fest days in the rural community proved to be the perfect spot for her to while away an hour on her own.

It was only one mile off the exit for the prison and a world away from James Haggard. Not that she hadn't thought Winding Creek was a world away from scum like him until he showed up there.

She pulled her phone from her handbag and checked for messages she might have missed. There were none. Hopefully that meant no more destruction of her bakery. She made a quick call to Crystal to satisfy herself all was well on that front, too. She spoke to Constance, as well.

The conversation lasted about two minutes, which was all the time Constance could spare from the day's adventure. Hiking was done. Next up was hamburgers and chocolate shakes.

Feeling mellower and more relaxed than she had in days, Dani stopped at a pottery display, immediately captivated by the brilliant colors of the glaze. She picked up a gorgeous pitcher in shades that ranged from sand to a dazzling turquoise.

"That's one of my favorite pieces," the lady standing inside the open stall said. "The glaze is lead-free and safe for all types of food and beverages."

"It's exquisite. Did you make it yourself?"

"I made everything that's on display, all one-of-a-kind."

Dani's thoughts jumped circuits, quickly switching to business. Several of the pieces on display now would not only add a touch of real class to the bakery's decor, but also likely be moneymakers for her and the artist.

"My name's Dani Boatman and I own Dani's Delights in Winding Creek."

"Really? I've heard of your shop from some of my customers. Best chocolate croissants and cinnamon buns in Texas."

"Maybe I should have that painted on my window."

"I'm Judy Kates. I also paint signs and windows."

In minutes, they'd made an appointment to discuss a business arrangement and Dani had purchased the pitcher for a thank-you gift for Esther after their ranch stay. The pitcher was so heavy she left it with Judy to be picked up when Riley called and said he was waiting for her at the exit.

As she walked away, she was surprised to realize that despite James Haggard's threats, despite the fact that she had no guarantee how the paternity testing would come out, she was still making plans for her and Constance to have a life in Winding Creek.

Riley's confidence had to be playing a role in that. His masculinity and virility screamed self-assurance. His protectiveness gave her the freedom to have faith in herself. His...

His rambling ways meant that he wasn't a forever type of guy.

He was who he was. Here and now. That would have to do.

She picked up a few more items—beautifully illustrated books about horses for Constance and Jaci, a jar of jalapeno jelly for Riley and a teal Western shirt with pearl snaps for herself.

Her phone rang as she paid for the shirt. She wasn't expecting Riley to be back for at least another half hour. She checked the caller ID. Unavailable.

Her throat tightened, and her hello sounded ragged even to her ears.

There was a moment of silence. She started to break the connection.

"I'm sure your cowboy lover will like you in that shirt."

The voice was unfamiliar. Anxiety ran roughshod through her veins.

She looked around, expecting to see James Haggard. When she didn't, she suddenly felt as if every man around was staring her. "Who is this?"

"It doesn't matter. I know where you went today. A waste of your time. I could have told you how the test results will come out. Get the money ready for James or start planning your life without any contact with your niece. That's not a threat, it's a promise."

# Chapter Thirteen

Riley looked through the rectangular piece of glass that separated him from Dudley. The man in prison orange was barely recognizable as the man Riley remembered from a short visit to the Double K Ranch about four summers ago. The man was likely around seventy. He could easily pass for eighty.

Riley had gone fishing with Charlie and Dudley in a stocked pond on Dudley's sprawling ranch. They'd caught a few bream and trout, but mostly the two old friends had guzzled beer and swapped stories from the old days.

Both men were ranchers, and there the similarities had ended.

Dudley Miles was probably the wealthiest guy in the county, his riches coming from his success in ranching and his wife's enormously large inheritance from her father's oil business. Millie loved their extravagant lifestyle. Dudley liked his cattle.

To look at the gaunt angles of Dudley's face and the loose bags of pale skin below his eyes and chin now, you'd assume Dudley hadn't enjoyed anything in decades.

The guard walked away. Dudley stared questioningly until the light of recognition reached his pale blue eyes. "Quick Draw." His lips twitched but didn't quite form a smile. "Wasn't expecting to see you here."

It had been years since anyone called Riley by the nickname Dudley had given him the first time he and Charlie took the brothers shooting.

"I'm in town for Pierce's wedding. Just thought I'd drop by and say hi."

"I appreciate that. Not many do, but I don't blame them. No good reason for it. Nothing changes in here. Nothing to talk about."

Dudley reached up and ran his wrinkled fingers through his thinning gray hair. "I heard about the wedding."

"I suppose Angela told you."

He shook his head. "No reason for her to come here. Wouldn't be good for either for us. Millie says Angela is dealing with the grief in her own way."

Riley doubted if Millie had told him that meant falling all over every guy who gave her a second look and some who didn't.

Looking at Dudley now, it was hard to imagine he could have a daughter close to Riley's age. But according to Charlie, Dudley had married late and it had taken Millie years to carry a baby full-term. Supposedly that explained why Angela had been known at school as a spoiled, stuck-up snot.

None of that was what had brought Riley to the prison today. Might as well cut to the unpleasant chase. "I have to admit I'm not just here to say hello."

"Didn't figure you were. I reckon you have questions about Charlie. Pierce did, too, when he drove down here to see me a couple of months back. Maybe more than a couple of months. Time doesn't seem to matter much around here."

And Dudley had a good chance of being here for the rest of his life.

"If I knew what got into Charlie, I'd tell you," Dudley said. "He never let on to me he was thinking about taking his life. If he had I would have found a way to stop him."

"Did he mention to you that he was having financial problems?"

"He admitted times were hard. They were for most ranchers after the big drought. I offered him money. A loan. A gift. Hell, I would have given him the shirt off my back. You know that."

"He turned you down?"

"I reckon he did. To tell you the truth, I don't remember much about what was going on back then. Had my own problems. My grandson…" Dudley's voice broke and he looked away.

"Want to talk about that?"

"No." He drew his lips together as if he was forcing the words to stay inside them.

He was hurting bad. Even Riley could see that. He could buy that Dudley had a couple of drinks and then fell asleep on the couch when he should have been caring for a toddler. What he couldn't bring himself to accept was that Dudley took that boy's dead body and tossed it into a woody area to rot.

"What really happened that day your grandson went missing, Dudley? We both know you'd never dump his body and then say he was kidnapped."

Dudley covered his face with trembling hands. He stayed that way for what must have been a full minute. Finally, he lowered his hands and spread them out, palms down, on the small table where he'd been resting his elbows.

He stared at them, avoiding eye contact. "It happened like I said. Now get out of here, Riley, and don't come back. Not you or your brothers. Life is over for both me and Charlie. Get out there and find your own life."

Dudley stood and strode away as if he was in a big hurry to get somewhere.

He'd been lying. Definitely about himself. Maybe about Charlie, as well. Riley likely wouldn't be around long enough to get to the bottom of this, but someone should.

*Get out there and find your own life.*

The essence of Dudley's order echoed through Riley's mind as he walked the long tiled corridor to the exit.

He'd thought that was what he'd been doing for

years. Traveling the world. Taking risks. Never settling. Finding his own life.

Yet here he was, back in Winding Creek, and all
he wanted to do was get back to Dani.

RILEY PULLED INTO the pickup lane near the gate to the
fairgrounds. He spotted Dani almost immediately,
her arms full of packages, her coppery curls catching the afternoon sun rays.

He got out of the car and waved. It wasn't until
she'd started in his direction that he noticed how
upset she looked. No smile. No rhythmic sway to
her shapely hips.

He helped her load the packages into the backseat
and then held the door for her.

He waited until he was seated at the wheel before
questioning her. "What's wrong?"

"Am I that easy to read?"

"No, I'm that talented a reader. Judging from
those packages, including the one you're still cradling like a precious treasure, you enjoyed the shopping. And yet you're still not smiling."

He eased into traffic as the car in front of him
pulled forward.

She looked around, turning so she could see out
the back window. "I'm being followed."

"You mean someone followed you around the
booths?"

"I mean someone has apparently been following
us ever since we left Winding Creek this morning."

He grew madder by the second as she shared the details of the alarming phone call.

"Are you certain the caller wasn't Haggard disguising his voice?"

"If it was, he did an excellent job of it."

"He may have hired a private detective to take over his dirty work for him. Not that he gained much from following us around all day."

"He knows we visited a lab."

"That shouldn't come as any surprise except that Haggard may not have realized you have a sample of his DNA."

"I still don't like the ideas of being stalked."

"I agree. I think it's time we do a little snooping of our own—find out everything we can about James Haggard. His past might prove him so unfit to be a parent that no judge would ever grant him custody of Constance."

"After some of the bizarre rulings I've read about, it's still risky trusting judges. But I'm game," Dani admitted. "I don't suppose you know any private detectives."

"Better. Pierce has a close friend with the FBI. Andy Malone, an old SEAL buddy. I know he helped out when Grace was in danger. He might be able to run a check and find something on Haggard, especially if has a criminal record. I'll talk to Pierce tonight and run the possibility by him."

"I'd like that, but about my staying at the ranch—"

"I already don't like where this is going."

"I'm being followed, Riley. I can't take this kind of trouble to the Double K Ranch."

"Are you going to sit there and tell me that you don't think Pierce, Tucker and I can handle the worst of what James Haggard can dish out?"

"I didn't mean it like that."

"You did. I'll forgive you this once. Don't let it happen again or we'll have to titillate you with thrilling recaps of Pierce's Navy SEAL exploits and videos of Tucker's mastery over a ton of bucking bull. If that doesn't do it, I'll demonstrate my legendary quick-draw skills."

"This isn't a joking matter, Riley."

"I'm not joking. It's all set. You and Constance need this vacation. Either you go with me willingly or I'll have to hog-tie and drag you there. Your call."

"Do you really want us there in spite of everything?"

"I've never wanted anything more." And that scared him a thousand times more than threats from James Haggard ever could.

IF DANI HAD any remaining doubts concerning the Double K vacation, they disappeared the second she saw the excitement in Constance's eyes as Jaci, Esther and Grace came running out to the car to welcome them.

"We're staying two days and two nights," Constance announced ceremoniously as she reached back into the truck for her backpack.

"Everybody's here," Jaci said, clapping her hands. "It's a giant slumber party all over our house."

"It's a vacation for us," Constance amended. "We're going on a trail ride."

"I know," Jaci said. "Mommy told me. I'm riding Dreamer. And guess what?"

"I can't guess what I don't know. You have to tell me."

"You can sleep in my room just like after the wedding."

"Except this time there better be more sleeping than giggling or you'll be too tired for an early morning trail ride," Esther warned.

The girls ran ahead.

"I swear to goodness," Esther exclaimed. "Those girls are quicker than jackrabbits and have more energy, too. Grace, why don't you show Dani to the bedroom with the private patio? I'll show Riley to the sleeping alcove off the back porch."

"What, no patio for me?" Riley asked.

"In town three days and you've yet to put your head on one of my pillows. You're lucky to get a bed, young man. If you'd been doing anything besides helping out Dani, you'd have gotten a pile of hay in the barn."

Riley put an arm around Esther's shoulders. "Aw, c'mon, admit it. You know I'm your favorite."

"I don't have any favorites among my boys, but

come around more often and you might work up to a room with a view of the woodshed."

"You have no heart."

Dani followed Grace to the end of the west hall. Grace opened the door and they stepped inside.

"Wow," Dani said. "I wasn't expecting this. A Queen Anne four-poster bed that looks so inviting I think I could melt in it. An antique dresser. The beautiful brass lamp. Fresh bluebonnets in a milky white vase. I had no idea Esther collected antiques."

"The furniture was all handed down from her maternal grandmother. She likes the part of her house where she says the living goes on to be simple. She keeps her treasures, as she calls her heirlooms, in the seldom-used guest rooms."

"I'm impressed."

"Be sure and let her know. She'll be delighted." Grace dropped to the edge of the bed. "What's the latest with your problems with James Haggard?"

"How much do you know?"

"Only what Riley has had time to tell Pierce."

"I feel terrible that my problems cut into your honeymoon," Dani said.

"Don't give it a second thought. I know it sounds a bit pretentious, but every day with Pierce is a honeymoon. I love him so much. I seriously can't put how happy he makes me into mere words."

"That's a powerful endorsement of commitment."

"So, back to the subject. Did you get the DNA to the lab today?"

"I did."

"I'm glad you came to the ranch with Riley."

"To be honest, I tried to back out, but Riley insisted."

"I'm glad you caved in. This much I know—the Lawrence brothers stick together and James Haggard will not get the best of them. Remember that Pierce's bravery and fast thinking are the reasons I'm alive today."

"I think Riley must have those same protective genes."

"He's a great guy, but Pierce says he's a rambler. Definitely a man you can depend on in a jam, but perhaps not a man to hitch your star to."

"So I've heard."

"I know. You heard it from me, but I don't want you to get hurt. You don't deserve a broken heart."

"I'm not going to fall for him."

True, she already had done so. That didn't mean she expected a miracle, or that she'd let Riley or anyone else make the final decision about how to best keep Constance safe.

DANI WALKED CONSTANCE back to bed for the third time in the last hour.

"I know how excited you are about all the fun activities you and Jaci have planned for the next two days, but if you don't get some sleep you'll be too tired to get up for the trail ride in the morning."

"I know, but I was too thirsty to sleep."

She was extremely creative when it came to excuses for prolonging bedtime. First her thumb had itched. Then her sheet was too twisted.

Constance stopped at the bedroom door. "I wish we had a ranch with horses and chickens and four-wheelers to ride through the mud."

"Who would I sell my pastries to?"

"We could still have the bakery. Some people have two houses. Bridget's family has a beach condo. They're there this week."

"But they don't have a bakery. I'll make a deal with you, though. It stays light a lot longer in summer. We'll try to come out to the Double K Ranch more often to ride horses."

"And feed the chickens?"

"And feed the chickens," Dani agreed. "Right now you need to get some sleep. And we have to be very quiet not to wake Jaci."

Constance nodded and put a shushing finger to her lips as she eased open the door. She tiptoed across the wood floors in her bare feet, then climbed into bed and crawled between the sheets.

Dani straightened the comfy coverlet and tucked it beneath Constance's chin. "I love you, sweetie," she whispered.

"Love you, too."

Dani kissed her good-night and Constance closed her eyes, hopefully this time to fall into a deep sleep colored with sweet dreams.

Her niece's life had never been easy before she

came to live with Dani. Without the intervention of Health and Human Services on more than one occasion, she might not even be alive.

Dani had never been given the chance to make a difference then. Now she had. Biological father or not, James Haggard would not rob Constance of happiness—not as long as Dani was alive to stop him.

The house was whisper-quiet when Dani left the girls' bedroom. Esther might have retired for the night, but the others were more likely outside catching up on each other's lives. It was practically the first time Riley had managed any bonding time with his boisterous brothers.

She definitely wouldn't barge in on that. A shower and early to bed actually sounded good. She might have needed this time away as much as Constance.

She stopped off in the kitchen for a glass of water for herself. The back door swung open, letting in a cool breeze and a grinning cowboy who sent her senses whirling.

"We were starting to wonder what happened to you."

"Constance was resisting bedtime."

Riley reached into the fridge for some beers. "Maybe I should go back for my guitar and play her a little George Strait."

"Like that wouldn't have Jaci and Constance both up and ready to dance. Actually I think they're both sleeping now, so let's leave it that way."

"Does that mean you're ready to join the party that's going on outside?"

"I was thinking I'd take a shower and hit the bed."

"I like your idea better. Your shower or mine?"

"Nice try, but I don't think that's in keeping with the rules of the house." Not that the offer wasn't titillating.

"I don't do rules. Did I not mention that?"

"You've given a few indications."

"What'll you have? Beer? Wine? Margarita on the rocks?"

"As a chaser for the margaritas I had earlier?"

"That was hours and one of Esther's five-thousand-calorie meals ago."

"I hate to crash a family gathering especially after stealing you from your brothers for days."

"They'll probably thank you for that. Besides, it's not like we're shaking old family skeletons around. We're mostly jamming out a little and laughing a lot."

"In that case, make mine a light beer."

"Got it." He pulled another bottle from the fridge.

"Let me grab a wrap and I'll help you carry those."

"Forget the wrap. The temperature's dropped several degrees, but we've got a campfire roaring. If that's not enough, my denim jacket's out there somewhere. And don't worry about the girls. Esther will hear them if they wake up and call for anyone."

She fell in step with Riley as they left through the back door and closed it behind them. The smell of smoke and the sound of laughter led them to the impromptu party.

Pierce and Grace shared an oversize lawn recliner and were entwined like the lovebirds they were. Grace had kicked off her shoes and tossed a red sweatshirt over her feet.

Tucker was in a folding lawn chair next to them, his booted feet stretched toward the fire, a banjo around his neck. There were two more chairs in the circle, one holding a guitar, one empty. She might not be wanted, but she'd evidently been expected.

She exchanged greetings and took the empty chair. Riley passed around the beers, then picked up his guitar and dropped into the chair next to hers.

"What did I miss?" Riley asked.

"Truth or lie," Tucker said.

"Ugh, I came back too soon."

"But you lie so well," Pierce said.

"I'll sit this one out a round or two until I get the hang of it," Dani offered. She wasn't a legitimate part of the family and she was a terrible liar, a virtue that sounded as if it would work against her in this game.

"Your turn, Tucker," Pierce said. "What's the least amount of time you stayed on a bull during a rodeo event?"

"Six seconds."

"Lie," they all shouted at once.

"You're right. It was seven."

"Lie."

"You gotta make music." Grace threw out a song title. "'Won't You Come Home, Bill Bailey.'"

Tucker jumped into the song on his banjo. Riley strummed a few hot chords on his guitar. Pierce pulled out a harmonica and joined in.

To Dani's surprise, they were all good. Really good. Even more impressive, they were all having fun. Surprisingly, so was she.

"Okay, Quick Draw," Grace said. "What's the longest time you ever stayed in one town?"

"That's easy. Winding Creek. Home, sweet home. I was here for almost fifteen years."

"I mean one town after you left college, rambling man," Grace clarified.

Dani couldn't help worrying if that question was for her benefit. She knew Grace meant well, but love didn't always come wrapped in neat packages. It had for Grace. Dani had no expectations that it would for her.

"Let's see," Riley said. "That would probably be Kentucky. I fell in love with a golden-haired beauty and couldn't bear to leave. Fastest two-year-old I ever worked with. I trained her so well I had hopes she might end up winning the roses."

"What happened?" Tucker asked.

"Boss's daughter didn't like being rejected when she threw herself at me. Lied and accused me of coming on to her. I got fired. Horse lost the race."

"How long were you there?" Grace asked.

"Eight months, give or take a week or two."

"I'll buy that as true," Grace said.

Riley grinned and played a run on the guitar. "Sucker. I've never lived in Kentucky and never trained a racehorse. I've thought about it, though."

"Never believe a thing old Quick Draw says," Pierce said.

They went around a few more times. More lies than truth from all of them.

Tucker kicked at a log, stirring up a few more flames before their fire died. "You haven't asked a question yet, Dani."

"I have one for Quick Draw."

"Sorry. Out of time," Riley teased.

"Where did you get the name Quick Draw?"

"So happens I got that name by using my considerable skills with a very large gun to save my brother's life."

Tucker groaned. "Here we go again."

"Dudley Miles and Charlie were giving Tucker, Pierce and me a shooting and gun-safety lesson. I won't go into all the details, but as usual, I was catching on faster than my brothers."

Pierce and Tucker booed on cue.

"We'd put the guns on safety. Tucker and Pierce returned their guns to our instructors. I slid mine into the holster I had buckled above my hips and took a few steps away from the group."

"The next thing we heard was his gun firing in rapid succession," Tucker said.

"Followed by Charlie yelling at me. All I'd done

was aim my pistol at a humongous rattlesnake lying dead less than a foot from where Tucker was standing. The viper had been ready to strike when I spotted him. If I'd yelled, Tucker would have jumped and the snake would have nailed him. So my quick draw and even quicker thinking saved Tucker's life."

Riley stood and took a bow.

"Lie," Dani said, sure she'd been taken.

"Tsk-tsk. How can you look into these honest eyes and doubt me?"

"It was the truth," Tucker said. "I could never forget that day, especially since Riley misses no opportunity to remind me."

They all laughed. For brothers who spent so little time together, they seemed exceptionally close.

Perhaps it was the shared tragedy of losing their parents. But Dani suspected it was also the experiences and love they'd shared with each other and Esther and Charlie Kavanaugh right here on the Double K Ranch.

"If I'm going to make a sunrise trail ride, I'd better head to bed," Grace said.

"Same here," Tucker said. "You guys may be used to ranching hours, but we bull riders sleep in till noon and tend our bruised and aching bodies."

"And draw the big paychecks," Pierce said.

"Only when we win."

Dani stood with the rest of them. Riley reached up, took her hand and tugged her back down beside him. "We'll stick around and see that the fire is fully out."

Truth or lie.

The question was, did she dare stay?

Her heart answered that one for her as she snuggled by his side to watch the fading glow of dying embers.

She might never have forever, but she had now.

## Chapter Fourteen

Winding Creek, Texas. The Double K Ranch. Home again. Nothing like what Riley was expecting when he'd made the long drive down from Montana.

It was always great getting together with his brothers, except that it brought back the heartbreaking moments along with the good. And with this visit was the added sadness of Charlie's death.

Riley knew without Esther saying it that she was walking around with a huge hole in her heart, one that could never be filled. He saw it in her eyes when Charlie's name came up in the conversation, heard it in her voice when she spoke of him.

It was life. No matter how much you loved someone, you could lose them forever in a heartbeat. That message was set as firmly in his mind as if it was engraved in stone.

And yet staring into the fire with Dani's hand in his, Riley felt a whirlwind of emotions roaring inside him, and not one of them had him wanting to back off.

If that weren't bad enough, his protective urges equaled the ones his libido was fueling.

He stood, took the guitar from around his neck and set it in his chair. "Let's move to Pierce and Grace's spot," he suggested. "More room to get comfortable."

He sat down first, scooted to the back of the wide lounger and spread his legs so that she could sit between them. He wrapped his arms around her waist and pulled her close so that her back rested against his chest.

He nuzzled her neck, intoxicated by the flowery fragrance of her perfume. "I've been dying to hold you ever since you walked out here." He nibbled and sucked her earlobe. "You take my breath away."

"You're too easy to impress."

"Not true. But whatever it takes to turn me on, you rock it, baby."

"You must have a fetish for plump chicks."

"What?"

"A fetish for plump chicks or chubby thighs."

He laughed out loud. He couldn't help it. The comment was so far off true it would have blown the motor out of a lie detector test. "Where did you ever get the idea you are plump? Do you never look in a mirror?"

"All I have to do is look around me at the size zeros, twos and fours, the sexy young women who look as if their skinny jeans were painted on them and they haven't had a chocolate croissant in their lives. They don't even take cream or sugar in their coffee."

"Pity the men who have to eat their cooking. You're not skinny, Dani. I'll give you that. You've got curves in all the right places.

"Like here." He cupped her breasts with his hands and felt himself grow hard as her nipples pebbled and arched at his touch.

"And here." He slid his hands to her hips. "And for the record, you have got the best-looking butt in at least seven counties, and that's without having your jeans painted on. Though I'll be glad to supply the paint and brushes if you want to try that."

"I'll keep that in mind, Picasso."

He readjusted her in his arms so that his lips could find hers. Once he started, he couldn't stop. He ravaged her mouth as his hands slid along her abdomen and his fingers worked their way between her thighs. Even through the denim, he felt the heat and imagined her getting slick and ready for him the way he was burning hot for her.

He covered her hands with his and led them to the aching swell of his erection. She massaged the length of his hardness through the rough denim of his jeans. His blood pulsed fast and hard. His breathing was clipped, his voice husky when he moaned her name.

She pushed away quickly. "Not here," she murmured. "Not yet. Not like this."

He struggled for breath and relief from the frenzied

hunger that had taken over his brain. "I'm sorry. I didn't mean to come at you like a wild man."

"Please, don't apologize. It wasn't what you did—what we did. It's just that so many people are around. Someone could walk out that door any minute. I think the wisest move for me right now is to go inside and go to bed—alone."

"This is a huge ranch. We can find a place to be alone."

"Not tonight. Not here. Not yet."

"Then at least let me walk you to your room."

"Not a good idea. Just stay out here and put out the fire."

"You just did that for me."

"I have no doubt you can get it roaring again when the time is right."

He watched her walk away. Fat? Hardly. Every inch of her looked fantastic. Every inch of her cried out to be made love to.

What was the longest he'd ever been in one place? Truthfully, he didn't know. He'd just always known when it was time to move on.

It definitely wasn't now.

IT WAS EIGHT in the morning when they stopped for breakfast in a grove of pecan trees. They'd traveled slowly on a short, easy path that was safe enough for Jaci and Constance to ride single.

Pierce helped Jaci from the saddle and tethered her mount. Riley did the same for Constance, who was as excited as Riley had ever seen her. Both girls went running to meet Esther, who'd driven up in the truck with the food and cooking utensils.

Jaci wasn't quite six, but she already looked like a natural in the saddle, especially riding Dreamer, the calmest horse in the stalls. Constance was older but not as experienced, since she didn't get the chance to ride nearly as often. She'd improve quickly with a little more time in the saddle.

Pierce walked over to the truck, where the other two guys were hauling out a camp stove.

"Thanks to Esther there's not a lot of preparation left to do," Pierce said. "The sausage is scrambled. Potatoes are diced and fried. All we have to do is scramble the eggs in with the sausage and potatoes and heat the tortillas while chugging down a mug of coffee and making it appear like we're working hard."

"I'll pour the coffee," Tucker said. "Shall I serve the ladies?"

"Sure. Nothing bur five-star service on the Double K Ranch. Thermos is in the back of the truck."

Pierce started cracking eggs. "We didn't get much chance to talk privately yesterday. Any new developments with James Haggard?"

"Not directly." Riley told him about the stalker call.

"Strange," Pierce said. "Was she sure it wasn't Haggard disguising his voice?"

"I asked the same thing. She assured me she was as certain as she can be from a phone connection."

"He may have hired a private eye, but I don't see the point of that. In fact, none of his actions make much sense. If he's the father, prove it. He can't expect to make a million-dollar deal with Dani without proof. Even if his name was on the birth certificate, that wouldn't prove anything."

"Which makes me question if there's a reason he doesn't want his DNA information revealed," Riley said.

"Like a criminal record?"

"Exactly." Riley started heating the tortillas in an iron skillet while Pierce stirred the eggs into the sausage and potatoes that had been warming as they talked.

"You may be on to something," Pierce agreed. "At the very least there may be an event in Haggard's past that would prevent any judge from granting him custody or even a token amount of the insurance settlement. That would leave threatening Dani into just handing over the cash his only chance of financial gain."

"I hate to ask," Riley said, "but are you still in touch with your old SEAL buddy who's with the FBI?"

"Andy Malone. He's working out of Florida, but he came through for me big-time when Grace was in danger. I'll give him a call right after we get back to the house. He may not get back to me immediately, but I'll let you know as soon as he checks out Haggard."

"I appreciate that, more than you know."

"Seems like you're getting into it pretty deep with Dani."

"Is that a problem?"

"Not for me. Grace is a little worried you'll break her heart."

"Isn't anyone worried about my heart?"

"Nope. I just hope you have enough sense to know when it's time to lay it all on the line. Take it from me, love done right is as good as it gets."

"I'll keep that in mind."

THEY WERE GETTING ready to mount the horses again for the last half of the trail ride when Dani's cell phone rang. She hesitated to even check the caller ID. It would be unbearable to discover that yesterday's stalker had followed her here.

"Aren't you going to answer that?" Grace asked. "It could be important.

"I just hate to take a chance on a call spoiling our perfect morning."

"Don't worry. We'll have lots more. You needed this and Constance is definitely getting horse fever. You won't be able to keep her away."

The phone stopped ringing. Dani breathed a sigh of relief until it started again. This time she checked the caller ID. Her alarm company. She was bordering on severe paranoia.

She took the call and made arrangements to meet the repair tech at the bakery at eleven o'clock.

Riley walked over the second he noticed her on the phone. "Is everything all right?"

"Yes, except that I have to tell Constance there's a kink in our vacation plans."

"What kind of kink?"

She explained the situation and Grace didn't hesitate a second before coming to the rescue.

"I'll keep the girls busy. You get your alarm fixed and you'll be back at the ranch by early afternoon."

Dani groaned. "I am so taking advantage of all of you."

"It's Winding Creek. We take care of our neighbors. You have to love that about this place."

"We'll stop at the lumberyard up on the highway and pick up a new back door," Riley said. "If we leave as soon as we get the horses settled, I can install it and be out of their way before they arrive."

"I don't suppose it would do any good to say you don't have to do that," Dani said.

"You heard Grace. It's Winding Creek. I'd lose my native status if I failed to be a good neighbor."

"We can't have that."

Which meant she'd be alone at the bakery with Riley after the security technician left.

She'd lain awake half the night fantasizing about making love to Riley. This time if he wanted her, she wouldn't pull away.

JAMES HAGGARD LEANED back in the front passenger seat of the red sports car and smiled. "Really? Your dad's in prison. I like you better by the minute. What did he do?"

"Does it matter?"

"It might. Did he kill someone?"

"No. He'd never have the guts to do that."

"He's your dad. Where's your respect?"

"He's all right. He was always on my case. I got tired of the lectures. But he's fine. The other prisoners probably love him."

James whistled as Angela pulled up to a huge metal double gate supported by tall brick columns. The house he could barely see in the distance reminded him of a Southern plantation house he'd seen in Louisiana years ago. "Does all of this belong to your family?"

"Sure. It's the biggest ranch in the county or something like that."

"How rich are you?"

"I don't know. No one ever talks to me about things like that. I'm their precious Angel. It works."

"I thought your name was Angela."

"It is. Mom and Dad are the only ones who call me Angel."

"The dad who's in prison?"

"Well, yeah. Back when I was growing up."

"Is your mother home now?"

"I don't know. Don't worry. You won't have to

meet her. She goes ape if I bring friends home to get high. Gotta keep up appearances like there's anyone in this Podunk town to impress."

He wasn't sure what he was getting into, but he figured it was going to be a hell of a ride and he had nothing better to do.

The ranch road they were on veered off to the left. A narrow dirt and gravel road jutted off to the right. She kept going left.

"Let's go back and take the other road," Haggard said. "Better chance of not meeting up with any nosy wranglers."

"No. No one goes down that road. Not anymore."

"What's wrong? You're not afraid I'll turn into a big bad wolf if we get lost in the woods, are you?"

"Just shut up about that road. There's nothing down there but a ramshackle, rotting fishing camp."

"On a lake or a river?"

"Might have been a river once. Just a mostly dried-up creek bed now."

"Sounds like the perfect place to light up."

Angela hit the brakes and skidded to a stop. "Get out. I mean it. You go where I take you or get out and walk back to town."

"Hot damn! You sure look good when you're mad." And was probably as mean as a bobcat. He'd be sure to keep that in mind.

She finally stopped the car near a sparkling clear pond. Parked right out in the open, where any cowboy riding by could see them. She might be a little nuts.

Angela got out, popped the trunk and pulled out a quilt. She spread it beneath a tall swamp willow and motioned him over.

The second he settled on the quilt, she dropped down beside him and started ripping his shirt open. Buttons popped and flew in all directions.

"Whoa there, baby. We haven't even shared a joint yet."

"Are you here to party or not?" she demanded.

"I didn't know we were racing to the finish line. I thought we'd talk first."

"About what?"

"Your job at the bakery. When do you go back to work?"

"Thursday, I guess, if I bother to show."

"I need you to show and do a big favor for me."

"I'm not stealing from the register."

"It's nothing like that. All I need is for you to do some snooping around. Keep your eyes open for an official-looking document to arrive from Corinthian Court Lab in San Antonio. While you're watching for that, look for anything official with Constance's name on it—like a birth certificate."

"Why would Dani leave something like that lying around?"

"She won't. You'll have to sneak around. Go upstairs. Open a drawer or two. Check the file cabinet."

"What's in it for me?"

"I'll do your shopping for you, take all the risks like I did today."

"Whatever I want?"

"As long as you got the cash to pay for it," he assured her."

"You're not planning to do anything to hurt Constance, are you? You wouldn't try to kidnap her."

"I don't have to kidnap her. I'm her dad and that's a fact. Get me that birth certificate and I'll just have to grab her and go."

EVERY MUSCLE IN Dani's body tensed as Riley turned onto Main Street. She hadn't heard from yesterday's stalker again, yet all of a sudden she was sure he was near.

Watching. Waiting to…

She couldn't finish the thought. She had no idea what he was planning, but the same creeping fear she'd felt when she heard his voice yesterday skulked inside her now.

Whatever he wanted, it had to do with James Haggard, and that meant it had to do with Constance.

"You're awfully quiet," Riley said. "Is anything wrong?"

"I'm just thinking maybe you're the one who has it right. Don't put down any roots and then it won't hurt so much if your world goes up in smoke."

Her phone rang. She checked the caller ID. Unavailable. Her stalker had no doubt called to welcome her home.

"Who is it?" Riley asked as she hesitated to take the call.

"Unavailable."

"Ignore the ring. Don't give the pervert the satisfaction of knowing he's making you uneasy."

She scanned the area. "He's out there somewhere, likely planning his next sinister move."

"If he shows up at Dani's Delights looking for trouble, he'll get more than he can handle."

"You're not carrying a weapon, are you?"

"Yes, but I know my way around a pistol."

"I don't want a gunfight, Riley. I don't want you shot."

"Nor do I. Being ready for trouble is not the same thing as looking for it or even expecting it. At this point there's no reason to suspect Haggard's more than a cowardly, money-grubbing bully attempting to frighten you into giving in to his demands."

She knew many of the ranchers and wranglers kept a gun on them when they working. It was usually a rattlesnake they were looking to kill. She couldn't push the thought of deadly violence out of her mind. "Have you ever killed anyone?"

"Does a two-hundred-and-fifty-pound grizzly in attack mode count?"

She shuddered. "You came face-to-face with a grizzly?"

"Yes, ma'am. My friend Jack and I were fly fishing in a glacial stream in Alaska. Jack and I had seen bears before in that area, but when they'd show up, we'd just back away and let them have their fishing spot.

"That time we didn't see the bear until it came charging at my buddy. Fortunately, I was able to take the grizzly down seconds before he attacked. Admittedly I was shooting a lot more firepower than I have with me today."

Leave it to Riley to take her mind off her own problems if only for a few seconds. "Truth or lie?" she queried, though it didn't matter. Either way the story had served its purpose.

"Truth. Alaska is a magnificent state, almost like traveling to another world."

He passed Dani's Delights and kept going.

She tensed. "Why didn't you stop? Is something wrong?"

He reached across the console and pressed his hand against her thigh. "Everything's fine. I'm just going to unload the new door in the back."

She'd forgotten all about the extra-strength metal replacement door he'd bought and loaded into the bed of his truck at the lumberyard a half hour ago.

She was so anxious about the stupid stalker she couldn't keep her thoughts straight. Time to pull herself together the best way she knew how.

It was time to bake.

WITHIN MINUTES OF getting down to business in her immaculate, commercial-grade kitchen, Dani felt her nerves beginning to settle. It had been that way since she made her first batch of chocolate chip cookies as a little girl. In her mind, there was something magical about measuring, creaming, blending and folding in myriad ingredients to create something as beautiful to look at as it was to taste.

To lose her bakery would be like losing a piece of herself.

Normally she worked to the sounds of Mozart, Wagner, Bublé or Sinatra. Today she was working to the beat of hammers and the whir of drills. The sounds weren't the only things that were magnified with Riley around.

He added a new spice, a robust flavor that she'd never experienced before.

"Hate to interrupt the genius at work, but do you know if there's any leftover paint around here to match the door facing?"

She looked up to find Riley at the kitchen door in his worn jeans and sneakers, shirt off, thick, dark hair mussed and falling over his brow.

The carpenter's belt hung below his waist, the tools dangling past his hips. His bare chest was as bronzed as his face and the rest of his hunky, tanned body.

Her insides quivered. Her legs grew weak. Her mind was muddled. She held on to the edge of the counter as the full effect of his virility left her dizzy.

"What did you say?" she asked.

"I said, 'Wow, do you look good punching that dough!' Do you need help?"

"Sorry, sir, but I don't believe those tools you're sporting could sufficiently coddle my red velvet cupcakes."

"You might be surprised what kind of satisfying work my tools are capable of."

And once again it wasn't the time or place to find out. "The repair tech will be here any minute. He's already ten minutes late."

"Well, okay, if you'd rather wait for him, but I predict he'll be a big disappointment."

"Paint," she said, knowing she'd best cool the flirting before she lost all control. "You were asking about paint."

"Right. The woodwork and trim around your back door needs a touch-up. Did your painters leave any extra when they finished your bakery remodeling?"

"They left a few partial cans of paint. I'm not sure which colors. They're on the top shelf of the storage cupboard between the men's and ladies' restrooms. The key is in the drawer under the first register."

"Good. I'll check it out."

He turned and was gone. It was uncanny how James Haggard's threats and calls from a taunting stalker could have her totally on edge and still she was falling this hard for Riley.

Temporary or not as this relationship might be, she no longer could be ruled by caution. When the security alarm was up and running and she and Riley had the house to themselves, she'd let him know she was ready to finish what they'd started last night.

No promises or love or forever expected.

She had just slipped her croissants into the oven and was about to start on chocolate cupcakes for the girls when her front doorbell rang.

She rushed to usher in the alarm tech. The sooner he got started, the sooner he'd be out of here. She swung open the door.

"I realize your shop is closed, but it's urgent that we talk," the man standing there said.

"You're not from the alarm company?"

"No, I'm Elton Sheldon, James Haggard's attorney, and I think you know why I'm here."

## Chapter Fifteen

He was wrong. Dani had no idea why he was here. The rules seemed to change with James Haggard every day. First she'd had a week to pull a million dollars from a hat. The next night he'd vandalized the bakery, apparently just to let her know he shouldn't be taken lightly.

Next a hired stalker. Now he'd sent his attorney to add more pressure.

"Your client doesn't seem to know what he wants, so how could I possibly know what you want?"

"Let me make it clear, then. James is Constance's father. You could start by acknowledging that his name is listed that way on the original birth certificate. A birth certificate that should have been given to him along with custody of his daughter. He is the legal next of kin and you know it."

"His name is not on the birth certificate, which explains why he doesn't have a copy of it."

"We also know that you delivered a fake sample

of James's DNA to a lab in San Antonio to deliberately infringe on his rights."

"You are the one who was following me yesterday. Is stalking women part of your attorney duties?"

"Only when working with dishonest women who'll do anything to hold on to an innocent child's money."

"Go to hell." She was practically screaming, but she'd had enough.

"What's the problem?" Riley asked, appearing with his usual perfect timing.

Sheldon took a step backward, putting him closer to the door. Clearly he'd expected to find her alone so he could bully her into complying with James's demands before she received the lab report.

"This man claims to be James Haggard's attorney and he's basically calling me a liar and a sleaze."

"Is that a fact?" Riley asked as he took off his tool belt.

"He's also my stalker and he seems to be quite concerned that we made a visit to a lab."

"I've said what I have to say," Sheldon said. "Your fake DNA testing will prove nothing. Cooperate or lose Constance. Time is running out."

"Actually it just ran out," Riley said. "James Haggard isn't fit to father a rat. The two of you tried to pull off a million-dollar scam. You picked a victim way out of your league. I hope you enjoy prison life."

"Why, you..."

The attorney doubled his fists and came at Riley,

landing a punch to his jaw. Riley got in the second blow. Blood shot from Sheldon's nose and splattered his face and the front of his shirt. He staggered back, but managed to keep his balance.

Sheldon lunged for the tool belt Riley had shed, wrapping his fingers around the handle of a hammer and struggling to wrench it free.

Riley grabbed him from behind, ramming his knee into Sheldon's crotch. The lawyer turned white, looked as if he might faint and then twisted around and came at Riley again.

This time Riley delivered a solid blow to his right jaw. Sheldon stumbled for a few seconds, spitting out streams of blood, before he finally went down.

Dani opened the door, and Riley literally tossed Elton Sheldon to the street.

"You'll pay for this," the lawyer muttered through the blood dripping from his split bottom lip.

"Bring it on."

A crowd quickly gathered around Sheldon. He muttered a string of vile curses as he got to his feet and staggered away.

A few seconds later, Dani heard the scream of sirens. The police. An ambulance. Or both.

"I'm sorry I dragged you into this. I never expected things to go this far so quickly. I definitely didn't think an attorney would take things to blows."

Riley wrapped her in his arms and swayed gently, rocking her to him. She felt his warm breath on her neck as he whispered in her ear, "There you go, apologizing again for something you couldn't control. I doubt he's an attorney, but he came here looking for a fight. Only the cowardly skunk was expecting it to be with you—not me."

"Do you think he was arrested or taken to a hospital?"

"Either way, he won't stay long. He's not going to admit he got beat up while working a con."

"I guess we won't know for sure it's a total con until we get the DNA test results back," she said. "But if Haggard really believes the tests will come back positive, why not wait until I have the proof? Wait. That's it. Haggard knows the tests will come back negative. He's desperate because it's now or never for him."

Her spirits lifted. "The second I get those negative test results, I'm calling Cavazos. I hope Haggard's tried and sentenced. Prison life will be exactly what he deserves.

"Now you're talking." Riley sniffed. "Do I smell something burning?

"My croissants." She dashed for the kitchen. Too late. Burned to a smoky black.

Even that couldn't bring her spirits down now. The alarm repairman would come and go, and then she'd be alone with Riley. The time couldn't pass quick enough.

THE SECOND BATCH of croissants came out perfect. As many as Dani had made in her career, they should.

She rinsed her pans and skidded them into her oversize specialty dishwasher.

The dishwasher, like her bakeware, had been a real splurge, but well worth it. She'd invested with the thought that she'd be here until Constance graduated from college and perhaps beyond.

Over the past few days, she'd feared that dream might be lost. Now she had more reason than ever to believe James Haggard was just a nightmarish glitch in her life's plans.

She picked up her phone and called Grace to check on Constance. No answer. In spite of her newfound hope, she felt a shudder of apprehension. She tried Esther's number. Finally, a cheerful hello.

"Hi, it's Dani."

"I thought you might be calling soon. How are the repairs coming along?"

"The back door is hung and looks great and very sturdy. The repairman is putting the alarm system through its final tests."

"Then I guess I'll see you and Riley soon."

"We might be delayed a little while, a few small tasks to finish."

"You take all the time you need, dear."

"I tried to call Grace but didn't get an answer. Do you know where she and the girls are?"

"Sure do. They went to the new movie theater up by the consolidated high school. The one with six theaters, though I can't see why a living soul would need that many to choose from. I don't know what they went to see, but they were mighty excited."

"I'll owe Grace several free child-care days after this."

By the time she said good-bye and broke the connection, the alarm tech was tapping on her open kitchen door.

"It's all set up, including a few advanced tasks you didn't have before. Have you got a few minutes for me to show you how all the settings work?"

"Sure." A few minutes of talk and then time alone with Riley. She could almost taste the salty thrill of his kisses.

Assured she knew how to operate the new and improved security system, she saw the nice young technician to the door and went in search of Riley.

She heard him before she saw him. He was on the back staircase talking to someone on the phone. She stopped and turned around, not wanting to eavesdrop on his conversation.

She didn't get away fast enough.

"I am so ready to get out of here. I'll be there as soon as I can make it. Time to start chilling the wine."

She rushed back to the kitchen, her stomach churning, suffocating fingers clutching her heart. She had been mooning over Riley like a foolish schoolgirl all day. He couldn't wait to get out of here.

Tears burned at the back of her eyes. She blinked

repeatedly, forcing the tears not to fall. Why was she surprised? Grace had tried to warn her.

She couldn't even blame Riley. He'd been embroiled in her problems from the first minutes he arrived in Winding Creek. He'd had hardly a minute with his brothers or any of his old girlfriends from his high-school days.

He went with his instincts, knew when life got overly complicated it was time to move on. Apparently, where she was concerned, that time was now.

Riley joined her in the kitchen. "I think we've taken care of everything, including Elton Sheldon. Are you ready to roll?"

"You go ahead. The girls are at a movie with Grace, so there's no reason for me to rush. I'll take my car this time and be out in a while."

"That's a terrible idea."

"Why?"

"Because I promised Esther we'd be back early afternoon and I'm not leaving you here alone."

"Okay. But I'll drive my own car. I may need it tomorrow."

"I doubt it. I fear Esther and Grace are conniving to give you the full ranch experience tomorrow and to make sure you have at least one day of actual vacation."

"I love your family."

"They obviously feel the same about you and Constance. Only they think you are family. I'll load my tools in the truck and leave by the back door. You set the alarm and I'll follow you to the Double K."

And then he'd hurry off to see someone who was chilling the wine.

SETTING UP A seduction scene was new to Riley. He'd never been accused of being a romantic, though he wasn't a jerk about it. He just tended to go with the flow. When the moment was right and the woman was willing, he let the details work out for themselves.

This time was different. Dani was different. He knew he'd never forget their first time making love, and he wanted it to be just as memorable for her.

He'd already saddled two horses and filled his saddlebag with the necessities. Now he just needed to persuade Dani to go riding with him.

That might not be as easy as he'd expected. She'd been a tad standoffish since they made it back to the ranch—she had shrugged off his attempt to kiss her when he left to go ready their mounts.

He was counting on that having more to do with the visit from Haggard's dubious attorney than with something Riley had said or done. Not that he'd ever pretended to understand women.

It was a good fifteen minute walk back to the house from the horse barn. Riley made it in ten. Dani was on the front porch with Esther, who was talking a mile a minute. Dani was bent over a potted plant, pinching off dead blooms.

That sight alone was enough to get his juices pumping. It was hard to figure how some guy hadn't roped and tied her years ago. He figured it wasn't for lack of trying. Tough on a man's ego to come in second to a pile of dough or a bowl of batter. He was finding that out for himself.

"Afternoon, ladies." He tipped his hat as he climbed the steps to the porch and lolled against a support post.

"What are you still doing around here?" Esther asked. "Gorgeous spring day like this, a cowboy should be out on his horse." Her eyes twinkled. She loved playing conspirator, especially if she sensed a little romance was involved. She'd packed the snacks and chilled the wine.

"I'm looking for a riding partner," he said. "How about you, Dani?"

She looked surprised and maybe a tad suspicious. "I think I'll pass this time and stay here with Esther."

"Lordy mercy, don't let me hold you back," Esther urged. "I've been up since before sunup and I feel a nap calling me."

"The horses need to be ridden," Riley said. "Have two saddled and waiting. Be a help to me if you come along." If subtlety didn't work, he'd raise the stakes. She wasn't getting out of this one.

"I'm not an experienced rider."

"The horse is experienced enough for both of you. Besides, I saw you ride this morning. You were in full control."

"That was a short, easy ride."

"We're not exactly going to be galloping down a mountain this afternoon. You'll be fine."

"If you're sure."

"Wouldn't be standing here cajoling if I wasn't."

"Then give me a minute to kick out of these sandals and change into my boots."

"Don't forget your hat and you might want sunglasses, as well. We'll be short on shade."

"Isn't our Dani something special?" Esther said once Dani was out of earshot.

"She is that."

"You don't think she's in any real danger of losing custody of Constance, do you?"

"How did you hear about that?"

"I'm not as deaf as you guys think."

"Ah. Selective hearing. How much do you know?"

"That some lying creep is pretending to be Constance's biological father and is trying to blackmail Dani into giving him half of Constance's trust fund."

"That's it in a nutshell. But whether the creep is lying or not, I can't believe any judge would rule in favor of that jerk. I don't see Constance going anywhere."

"What about you, Riley Lawrence? Where are you running off to next?"

"Is that what you think I do, run off?"

"It is. First ill wind slaps you in the face and off you go, running to find what you don't even know you're looking for."

"Sounds like you've got it all figured out." Which was a lot more than he did.

"I think it's time you quit running. It won't protect you from bad moments in life. Nothing will. It might keep you from finding true happiness, though.

"All I wanted to do that day I found Charlie's body was run and never stop. Ran myself into a heart attack that I prayed I wouldn't live through."

"I'm glad you did," he said.

"So am I now. I still miss my Charlie every second of every day, but that don't keep me from knowing how blessed I am to have Pierce and Grace in my life. It don't keep me from lovin' and laughin' and getting downright soggy-eyed when Jaci gives me a hug and calls me Grandma. Don't keep me from loving it when you Lawrence boys are all at my kitchen table like the old days."

"I'll come back and visit more often. That's a promise."

"I'd like that, but I'm still saying that maybe if you stopped running around the country long enough and just looked around you, you might find that the best thing for your soul is right here."

He couldn't argue with that.

But what if he tried and everything went wrong? What if he made promises he couldn't keep?

Was that what he was setting himself up for now? If so, Dani deserved better than that.

Dani swung through the screen door that went on every spring to let the breeze in and keep the mosquitoes out. His brain screamed that he should run for the hills for both their sakes.

His brain was fighting a losing battle.

IT WAS A slow but steady climb up the sloping incline. Riley and his stately, chestnut-colored quarter horse led the way.

Dani loved riding behind Riley. She liked the tilt of his head and the sway of his body, seemingly in perfect harmony with his horse.

He looked like a man who owned the world and yet she knew he owned nothing except what fit in his truck when the need to roam hit him again.

They were opposites in so many ways. She felt most at home in her bakery. Rising before the sun to light her ovens and start rolling out her first batch of cinnamon rolls was balm for her soul.

That was not a portable life.

But she couldn't knock Riley's choices, either. Reveling in the view of rolling pastures, meandering creeks and myriad wildlife was more exhilarating than she'd ever imagined. If she lived to be a hundred, she doubted she'd ever tire of sharing moments like this with Riley.

Not that she'd ever get the chance to find out.

Riley reined in his horse as they left a cluster of cedar trees and entered a clearing. She followed his lead.

"This is a good place to give the horses a rest and let them drink their fill of water."

She looked around as he dismounted, her breath catching at the magnificent view. Off to the east were rolling pastures as far as she could see.

To the west was a slow-flowing stream. Riley led his horse there and tethered him to a low branch of a mulberry tree.

"The gorge at Lonesome Branch," Riley said as he helped Dani from the saddle. "Best view on the Double K Ranch."

The gorge. His special place. He'd bought her here to his special place. Emotion welled until she felt her heart was caving into her chest.

He tethered Dani's horse and then reached for her hand. "You haven't seen the best part yet."

"No, but I can hear the waterfall."

They walked together to the edge of the cliff. The water from the stream cascaded over layers of huge boulders and made a steep drop to the bottom of the gorge.

She stared at the drop-off, her mind painting the vivid image of Riley as a boy of fourteen poised on the edge of the precipice, struggling to come to grips with his fears and grief.

He was no longer that boy. He was every inch a man. Strong. Virile. Tough enough to face a grizzly. But somewhere inside that hulk of masculinity, a remnant of that frightened boy must still exist.

"I always compare this place to life," Riley said. "There's always a cliff waiting just around the corner. One false step and you plunge over the edge. That's why I go for the gusto. Do it all before you fall."

"I guess that worldview is okay if it works for you."

"What's yours? Maybe I'll adopt it."

She gave the question serious thought. "I suppose it's find the place that's home to your heart and then live life to the fullest, without regrets, every day."

"And that place for you is Dani's Delights in Winding Creek, Texas?"

"It definitely feels that way now."

He walked back to where the horses had waded into the cool stream. For a second, she thought he was upset with her and ready to saddle up and ride back to the house.

Instead of untying his horse, he reined it back to the bank and began unloading his saddlebag. By the time she joined him, he was spreading a lightweight blanket in a grassy area a few yards from the bank.

She grabbed one corner and helped him straighten it. He went back for two small tote bags. He set them on the blanket, hunched down and started unloading small containers of deviled eggs, veggie sticks, purple grapes, cheese and crackers.

"You come prepared."

"With a little help from Esther." He pulled out a bottle of white wine, uncorked it and filled two plastic glasses.

Dani's heart beat faster, her pulse climbing.

This was the chilled wine he'd ordered. He'd been talking to Esther. The wine was meant for Riley to share with Dani at the gorge at Lonesome Brach.

She was such a dope. Falling back into her old ways. Never really expecting guys to become serious about her. But she'd never felt about any other man the way she did about Riley.

She sipped her wine and then lay back on the blanket, her hands cradling the back of her head. Riley stretched out beside her and pulled her into his arms. When their lips met, she closed her eyes and melted into the thrill of him. This time there would be no pulling back.

Riley wasn't a forever guy, but the glow from their lovemaking would warm her soul for the rest of her life.

## Chapter Sixteen

Dani raised herself up on her elbow and laced her fingers through the fine hairs on Riley's sun-bronzed chest. His eyes were closed, his hat lying beside him. His naked body was dappled by late afternoon sun rays that penetrated the leafy branches that had been shading them for the last two hours.

They'd made love twice. The first time had been a delirious rampage of passion. He'd kissed, nibbled and sucked every inch of her body until she was so hot and slick with desire that she was begging to feel his erection inside her.

He'd swept her into an orgasm so intense that she'd felt as if her chest might explode. She'd lain in his arms for long minutes after that, totally spent, basking in the afterglow and thinking she'd never recover. A few grapes and another glass of wine were all it had taken to have her hungering for more of Riley's sweet kisses on her lips.

And on her neck. And on her breasts and her abdomen and the hot, slick pool at the triangle of her desire. The lovemaking had gone more slowly that time. He'd teased and tasted, brought her to the edge of ecstasy only to slow his rhythm again and again until she could take the sensual titillation no longer.

They'd exploded together in a frenzied eruption that rivaled the first time. And then sweet, honeyed contentment had flowed through her like warm cream.

There had been no soft whispers or throaty moans of love. She hadn't expected it. Riley was who he was. She'd been warned before they even met.

She was who she was, too. And she was a woman in love. How could she not be in love with Riley Lawrence?

THE WOMEN HAD cooked the evening meal. The men drew KP duty. It wasn't the way it had been when the Lawrence brothers lived here as teenagers. But even on the ranch, times had changed. No one complained.

Riley loaded the last of the dishes in the dishwasher as Tucker swept up and Pierce wiped down the counter.

"Anyone for a beer?" Tucker asked.

"Wouldn't turn one down," Pierce said.

Riley took three beers from the fridge and passed them around. The brothers settled back around the scarred kitchen table.

"Now that the women aren't listening, are you gonna tell us about the fight that is making your jaw a new shade of purple?" Tucker asked. "And then explain why we didn't get invited to the brawl?"

"To be honest, I didn't see it coming until I saw my obnoxious opponent's fist flying at me."

Riley explained the situation, assuring them he gave better than he got.

"I don't get the worry over a birth certificate," Tucker said. "DNA would take precedence over that in any court of law."

"As close as I figure, either Haggard knows the paternity test will come back negative or he fears it will," Riley said. "In which case he'll have as much chance at getting his hands on Constance's trust fund as he does at winning a spot on the Dallas Cowboys' roster."

Tucker rocked his half-empty beer bottle back and forth on the table. "So you see this as a desperation dance?"

"Most likely."

"Guess it was a gamble," Pierce said. "If it had worked and Dani had been so frightened by his threat that she'd paid off, he'd have been up a million."

"And that possibility was not as far-fetched as it sounds," Riley said. "If Haggard's name had been on the birth certificate and Dani could have gotten her hands on the money, she might have caved. That's how frightened she is at the thought of that conniving bastard gaining custody of Constance."

"And then she'd been opening herself to more blackmail," Pierce said.

"Nothing will be completely settled until you get the lab results," Tucker said. "And not even then if the results come back positive or maybe if it doesn't."

"Any word from your buddy with the FBI?" Riley asked.

"He called back to say he got the message and he'll see what he can find."

"That's all I can ask. I've been thinking more about my prison visit with Dudley Miles."

"Can't even imagine what came over that man unless he got into his daughter's stash."

Riley downed the last of his beer. "There's something fishy going on there. I can't figure it out yet, but I'm not giving up."

Tucker stood and gathered the empty beer bottles. "Unfortunately, I have to give up on all of you. I'll be out of here Friday morning and doing my damnedest to stay personal with an ugly bull for eight seconds on Friday night."

"You're heading out quicker than I expected," Riley said.

"And you're sticking around longer than I expected. Not that I blame you. Just saying. But I've got a proposition for both of you before I leave."

"Let's hear it," Pierce said.

"I'm challenging you to a brother-against-brothers chili cook off tomorrow afternoon. You don't have a chance of winning, but the challenge will do you good."

"Count me in," Pierce said. "Ten dollars to the winner. I love taking you guys' money."

"I'll be here unless something develops with the continuing Haggard saga," Riley said. "See you then if I don't catch up with you before that.

"Where are you off to in such a hurry now?" Tucker asked. "Oh, never mind. Sorry I asked."

Riley grinned.

It was great hanging with his brothers, but it was Dani he wanted to be with now.

JAMES HAGGARD WOKE up on the side of a country road behind the wheel of his old pickup truck. He groaned and grabbed his head, pressing hard against his hammering temples. He had no idea where he was or how he'd gotten here.

His truck smelled like vomit and sweat. He poked his head out the window and gulped in the clean air.

Revived a little, he worried the handle until he got the door open. He stepped outside, then grabbed on to the door as his head went spinning. It wasn't daylight, but it wasn't the pitch-black of night, either.

His right leg started to cramp. There was no way of knowing how long he'd been crunched up beneath the wheel.

Using the truck for support, he worked his way to the passenger side and then staggered into the woods to relieve himself.

Something scurried over his foot. He jumped and then fell backward, landing on his rump. Whatever he'd inhaled, injected or drunk with crazy Angela, he never wanted to touch again.

He sat there in the underbrush with mosquitoes buzzing about his face, and his stomach and head taking turns with the torture.

Slowly, disjointed bits and pieces of information popped into his consciousness. Something about a toddler buried in the woods. Crying that wouldn't stop. A kidnapper. None of it made any sense.

The night grew darker. Finally James staggered back to his truck and passed out.

The next thing he knew, some frigging idiot was slapping him over and over in the face.

He opened his eyes as much as he could, which was only a slit. His brother was staring down at him.

"Stop hitting me," James bellowed.

"Where the hell have you been? You smell like a latrine."

James tried to focus on Lenny's black eyes and misshapen face. "Somebody beat the crap out of you."

"Because I was out trying to get you the million dollars that tramp in the bakery stole from you. It's just like always, I try to take care of you and you just get drunk or high. I'm through saving you. You're not worth it."

"No. Don't be mad at me, Lenny. I'll do whatever you say. Anything. You're too good to me." His head kept pounding. He was going to be sick. Lenny would hit him again if he threw up.

"This is the thanks I get," Lenny said. "You can't even get your hands on the birth certificate for the kid you claim is your daughter."

"She's my daughter. Amber was crazy in love with me back then, same as I was about her. She would never have cheated. Not then. I'm sure of it."

That made one of them.

RILEY WOKE TO the smell of coffee and Dani's cinnamon rolls. He kicked off the sheets and reveled in the tender ache in his crotch and upper thighs.

In the hope of tamping down speculation, Dani had kicked him out of her bed and back to his bed before daylight this morning, but not before they'd made love for the fourth time in less than twenty-four hours.

Keep up that pace and he'd never be able to ride a horse again. Whatever kind of spell she'd cast on him, he hoped it lasted forever.

Forever?

He hadn't known that word was even in his internal vocabulary. He threw his legs over the side of the bed and headed for the shower.

It was the last day of her impromptu vacation. He wanted it to be special and free of visits or calls from Haggard or his crooked attorney.

Riley would love to hear from Andy Malone but only if it was good news, whatever that might be.

He ran the water in the shower until it was as hot as he could stand it before stepping under the spray.

He wasn't too keen on washing Dani's scent and love juices off his body, but that just meant he'd have to acquire them again.

Dani slid her second pan of hot cinnamon rolls from the oven. The original six had disappeared with the first pot of coffee. These should go slower, since Esther had just placed a platter of bacon on the table and Grace was busy frying fresh eggs.

Riley was the last to join them. His brothers immediately started ribbing him.

"About time you made it up, Quick Draw."

"Were you up all night researching losing chili recipes?"

"Are you kidding? I can beat you guys with chili made with my right hand behind my back."

"Ten bucks says you can't."

Riley poured himself a cup of coffee. "You guys will bet on anything."

"What are we going to do on my last day as a cowgirl?" Constance asked. "I hope it's ride the horses."

"I'm sure we can fit that in," Grace said.

"How about me taking the females to a high school female barrel-racing event?" Tucker suggested.

"What's barrel racing?" Constance asked.

"A rodeo competition. Both of you young ladies could be barrel-racing champions in practically no time if you worked at it."

"Yes," Constance squealed. "I want to be in a rodeo. I used to want to be a pastry chef like Aunt Dani, but now I want to be a cowgirl so I can live on a ranch and ride horses every day."

"What time's the competition?" Pierce asked.

"One o'clock," Tucker said. "We can stay awhile and easily be home in time for me to embarrass you two in the chili cook-off."

"I'm fixing to take a drive over to the Wallaces' spread and look at some Angus breeding stock he's looking to sell," Pierce said. "If either of you guys has the time to come along, I'd appreciate your input."

"How much stock is he selling?" Riley asked.

"All he owns, but I'm not interested in anything but the Angus. He's planning to sell off a few thousand acres of his ranch come fall if he can get a decent price for it."

"I don't remember the Wallace spread," Tucker said. "How would you rate it?"

"Excellent water sources and great grazing land. You and Riley should take a look at it. Consider going in together and buying it. You have to settle down somewhere one day."

"I might consider that," Tucker said. "Bull riding is not a job you can grow old in."

Not surprisingly, Riley didn't comment.

Dani was passing the bacon to Pierce when she saw him reach for his phone. He checked the screen, nodded to Riley and silently mouthed the name Andy.

Pierce left the room with Riley at his heels. She stood and hurried to follow them to the family den. This was her fight and she wasn't sitting it out.

# Chapter Seventeen

"Riley and Dani Boatman are here with me."

"Then put your phone on speaker. Nothing I have to tell you is classified."

"Ready on this end," Pierce said.

Dani scooted closer to the phone, not wanting to miss anything the FBI agent had to say.

"James Haggard has an arrest record that is miles long, though he's never served much time and hasn't been arrested in over five years. His crimes range from online scamming to unarmed robberies."

"Seems he's picked up his old habits," Riley said. "What's the possibility he could escalate to more violent crimes?"

"Not great, but you can never rule that out with a man like Haggard, especially with this amount of money involved. He's been a petty thief for the most part."

"It may sound like a lot of money," Dani reminded him. "But it's not as if someone can just write a check for it. It's in a trust fund."

"If you're a legal parent, there are always ways around that if you try hard enough," Andy offered. "The real danger is that the trust-fund money might lure James's older brother into the mix if it hasn't already. I wouldn't be surprised if he's behind Haggard's scam."

"What do you know about him?" Pierce asked.

"Have you ever heard of Cecil Molina?"

"Sounds familiar," Riley said.

"He runs the most profitable smuggling operation the Western Hemisphere has ever seen. Guns. Illegal drugs. Humans. An underage sex ring. He's active across South and Central America and on our southern border."

"Sounds like he spreads himself thin," Riley said.

"Which is why he's still at large. If he gets close to being caught in one area, he moves somewhere else."

"I'm not following this train of thought," Dani said. "What does Cecil Molina have to do with James Haggard or his brother?"

"Sorry," Andy said. "We FBI agents tend to get caught up in the big picture. Lenny Haggard *was* Molina's top hit man. Lenny is wanted for murder in Texas, Arizona and California. His last hit was a judge's family of five in south Texas."

"Sounds like he's probably pulling down his share of money on his own," Pierce said.

"He was, but we hear through very reliable sources that he crossed Molina and now Lenny is on Molina's hit list. He may have split the country by now, but there's a chance he's looking for funds to get him far away from Molina's large base of operations."

"Which would explain the desperation and the rush to settle with cash," Riley said. "And up the likelihood for violence."

"Let's just say Lenny has killed for a lot less," Andy said.

"Do you have a picture of Lenny?" Riley asked.

"On my computer, which is right here."

"Start the transfer anytime." In a matter of seconds, the pictures started popping up on the phone's screen.

"Son of a bitch," Riley muttered.

"Does that mean you recognize him?" Andy asked.

"Let's just say that if there's a price on his head, I'm ready to collect."

Riley explained the fact that Lenny was in Winding Creek and posing as James's attorney. "Do you want me to call the local sheriff?"

"Not unless you feel you're in immediate danger. Winding Creek will be crawling with FBI agents by the end of the day. Someone will call you back within the next half hour to find out everything you know. In the meantime, be careful and don't go near Dani's house until I give you the all-clear."

"I own a bakery," Dani protested. "I open for business at seven tomorrow morning and I have to be there at least three hours before that to start baking."

"If all goes well, that won't be a problem. We hope to have both James and Lenny in custody by then. If not, we'll get back with you on how to handle the situation with the bakery."

"You guys are damn serious," Pierce said.

"You got that right, especially when the suspects may lead us to Cecil Molina."

"Just think," Pierce said when they'd finished the call. "You beat up a real badass today, Riley. This may even replace your grizzly story for an attention grabber."

"And to think I could have held him until the FBI got there and really earned hero status."

Dani knew that they weren't taking this lightly, that it was just the way men handled things when they couldn't admit fear. She was afraid and didn't mind admitting it.

"No rodeo for Constance this afternoon," she said.

"Not a problem," Riley said. "There will be no rodeo for the others, either. We'll all stay here where you've got three bodyguards until the FBI makes an arrest. I don't expect that to take long."

Dani whispered a prayer as she went back to the kitchen, where she could be close to her precious niece.

*Please don't ever let either of the Haggards touch Constance's life. And please keep everyone safe.*

DANI WAS STRETCHED out in a yard chair next to Grace and Esther, a few yards away from where the girls were playing on the tire swing and a bit farther away from where the men were drinking beer and tending their pots of chili simmering over outdoor propane cookers.

The ringing of her cell phone startled her and a wave of anxiety coursed through her. She checked the ID. Sheriff Cavazos. As far as she knew, the FBI hadn't contacted him, so she was surprised at his call.

"Hello."

"Don't have the best of news for you, but hope I didn't catch you at a bad time."

"Just trying to relax. What's the news?"

"Cory Boxer is no longer a suspect in the vandalism of your shop."

No surprise there, at least not for her.

"He has an airtight alibi for the time of the break-in," the sheriff continued. "Turns out he didn't even actually break into Joe Clark's trunk."

That was a surprise. "I thought he was caught in the act."

"Caught in the act of snooping but apparently nothing worse. The lock on the truck wasn't broken and Joe Clark finally admitted that he might have accidentally left it open since he was planning on coming right back. Cory said he only ran off because Joe started yelling curses at him. At any rate, he's not your suspect."

She didn't tell him that she felt certain her vandal would be officially identified soon.

Another call came in only seconds after she broke the connection with the sheriff. This time it was the FBI with instructions as to how they wanted her to handle her end of the situation.

The shop and that entire block of Main Street would be under tight scrutiny tomorrow and they requested she open the bakery as usual. They didn't want the Haggards to suspect a thing if they approached Dani's Delights.

They assured her that neither Lenny nor James would be allowed to enter the bakery and that her customers would not be put in danger. She had no choice but to take them at their word.

"Good news, I hope," Grace said when Dani slipped her phone back into her pocket.

"As good as can be expected until I hear they've arrested both of the Haggards. I can open my bakery as usual tomorrow with the assurance the FBI has everything under control."

"Too bad we didn't think to call them sooner," Esther said.

"Even if we had, we wouldn't have gotten this kind of response before Lenny entered the picture, and that was only yesterday. I guess I should go and give Riley the latest news, though I hate to interrupt all that stirring and boisterous bragging he's doing over his big iron chili pot."

"I admit Riley's surprised me," Grace said. "I kept hearing about his rambling ways and I mistakenly interpreted that to be an unwillingness to grow up and take on responsibility. But he's really come through for you and Constance."

"All my boys have good hearts," Esther said. "I never want to see a one of them ride off in the sunset, as Charlie used to say. He also used to vow that the Double K Ranch was never more alive than when the three of them were here."

She reached up and wiped an unexpected tear from her eye.

"You must still miss your husband very much," Dani said.

"Too much. Don't ever waste a minute of the time you can share with the man you love. Once he's gone, you can never get him back. All you have left to cherish is the memories."

Dani agreed. She walked over to the cooking area and gave Riley a hug around the waist, burying her face beneath his broad shoulders.

"Guess the odor of my chili is making you crave my body."

"No. I just have a thing for men with big iron pots."

"You okay?" he asked.

"Yeah. I'm okay. Who can worry with you and the FBI in charge?"

When she got her next call she was taking a walk alone, trying to come to terms with all that happened over the last few days. This time it was the lab.

## Chapter Eighteen

"I'm calling for Dani Boatman."

"Speaking."

"This is Courtney Graves with Corinthian Court Laboratories. I talked to you when you were in Monday morning."

"I remember. Is there a problem?"

"No. We're open late on Wednesday evenings and I was just handed your finished report. You signed the permission form that you wanted to be notified by phone as soon as the report was finished."

"I remember."

"Are you ready for the results?"

"Yes. I didn't expect to hear before tomorrow, but I'm ready."

"The test came back negative for paternity."

The breath she'd been holding came out in a gush. "That was so what I wanted to hear."

"There's more."

"Like what?"

"The results are negative for paternity but positive for a familial relationship."

"What are you saying exactly?"

"The man whose blood was sampled is the uncle of the child."

"That can't be."

"I'm sorry the results are not what you were hoping for, but all we can do is give you the findings. You'll receive a written copy of this via FedEx possibly in the morning, but Friday morning by the latest."

So it was likely Lenny Haggard was Constance's biological father. The thought made her sick. But Constance was no more like Lenny than Dani was like what her sister, Amber, had been.

The news she had to hold on to was that this would all be over soon. She had the FBI's word on that. If she couldn't trust the FBI, who could she trust?

Dani hurried back to join Riley and the men. Perplexed and sick at heart, she just needed to be near him.

"TRY THIS," RILEY SAID, pushing a spoon of chili at Dani. She parted her lips for the tiniest taste.

Her mouth exploded in peppery fire.

"Water," she called, fanning her open mouth with her hand. "Water to put out the fire."

"She likes it hot," Riley announced loudly. "One vote for me."

She'd break the news about the test results after they had their chili. She'd already stolen too much of the brief time Riley could have spent with his brothers. She'd give him this reprieve and then they'd contact the FBI with the news that Lenny Haggard was Constance's biological father.

THE BAKERY OPENED as usual on Thursday morning.

"Such a shame about the break-in. I head they had to let that Boxer fellow go. Have they arrested anyone else?"

"Not that I've heard," Dani answered as she handed Mrs. Dupree her change.

"I hope they do soon. We can't stand for this kind of senseless crime in Winding Creek. We're all neighbors and we stick together."

"I agree. I'm sure the sheriff will arrest a credible suspect soon."

Her next customer, Jenny, another of her regulars, stepped up to the counter. "One of your delicious cinnamon rolls and a caramel latte."

"For here?"

"Yes. I'm meeting Sara Pendleton, but she's always late. If I order for her, it's never what she wants."

"Sara does like variety," Dani agreed.

"I can't tell you how disgusted I was when I heard about your break-in. The whole town is. I'm probably not supposed to mention this, but Sara's Bible study group is collecting money to help you recover your losses."

"That's extremely thoughtful, but really, I'm fine."

"It's the principle of the thing. We stand together just like we always have in this town. Let the criminals move in and first thing you know, the shops start moving out and Main Street becomes a ghost town."

"I'm not going anywhere," Dani assured Jenny as she topped off the latte with one dollop of whipped cream, just the way she liked it.

It had been like this ever since she opened the door at seven. A steady stream of customers. A steady stream of empathetic comments.

Everyone in town seemed to know about the vandalism. So far no one seemed privy to the fact that an infamous criminal was hanging out in their area or that the FBI had invaded Winding Creek.

Dani was almost certain the two men drinking their second cups of coffee at one of the back tables were agents. And there would be others observing the shop from locations on Main Street and the alley behind her shop.

Riley had spent the night. He'd been as shocked as she was by the news that Lenny was Constance's biological father. But even knowing that, he'd felt enough confidence in the FBI's protection that he'd left a few minutes ago to drop off Constance at school. Then he was making a quick stop at one of Dani's local suppliers to pick the freshest carrots for the carrot-cake muffins she'd be making later.

The bell above the door rang. This time it was Angela who strode in, wearing a clingy knit pullover, denim shorts that barely covered her behind and a pair of red Western boots.

She yawned and came over to the counter. "Sorry I'm late. My alarm didn't go off."

Improper attire. Not punctual. Zero motivation. Dani would have to fire her, but the last thing she needed this morning was a scene with Angela.

"You can start by clearing and cleaning the vacated tables," Dani said as she poured an espresso. "Make sure you don't leave them sticky and get all the crumbs from under the table or chairs."

"What do I wipe the tables with?"

"Clean white bar towels are on the wire shelves just inside the kitchen. The lobby sweeper for the floors is behind the far end of the counter."

Angela looked as if Dani had just asked her to scrub the floor with a toothbrush, but she did start clearing the tables. Dani went back to waiting on her customers.

The first break in business came just after Riley returned. That was also when she noticed that half of the tables in the shop still needed to be cleared. She looked around. Angela was nowhere to be seen.

Dani poked her head into the kitchen, where Riley was pulling bunches of carrots from reusable bags. "Can you watch the shop for a second?"

"No problem."

Dani marched to the back door, assuming Angela was taking a cigarette break. She opened the door and scanned the area. No Angela. No cigarette odor. No sign of FBI agents, but that didn't mean they weren't watching from somewhere.

As she stepped back inside, she heard what sounded like a door banging upstairs. She walked halfway up to the second floor. "Angela."

"Yeah. Up here."

Where she had no business being. Patience stretched to just past its limit, Dani took the rest of the stairs two at a time.

She heard the commode flush and found Angela at the open bathroom door. This time the smell of smoke was stifling. "This area is private and off-limits at all times."

"The bathroom downstairs was in use and I had to go bad. I didn't think you'd get all bent out of shape about that."

Maybe Dani was overreacting. Her nerves were ragged and strained.

Angela walked toward the staircase. Dani had started to follow when she noticed the door to her bedroom was open. She hadn't left it that way. She glanced inside and saw that half the drawers in her tall chest were open.

Her temper exploded. She raced down the stairs and grabbed Angela's right wrist. "I suppose you also have a reason for rummaging through my private belongings."

"I don't know what you're talking about."

"I'm talking about invasion of privacy. I want you

out of Dani's Delights and I never want to see you in here again. Never."

"You can't fire me over nothing."

"Get out, Angela. Now."

"Bitch."

Dani was seeing red, so mad she was shaking as she followed Angela into the bakery to make sure she left without breaking anything.

A customer was at the counter, but Dani didn't see Riley. She went back to the kitchen to check on him. He was calmly boxing cookies that she'd never had time to get to the display case.

"What's the problem?" he asked. "You look like you're ready to horsewhip someone."

"I just found Angela Miles going through the drawers in my bedroom."

"Did she take anything?"

"Probably not. My clothes would swallow her skinny body. I was so perturbed I fired her on the spot."

"You had to see that coming."

Riley tied a length of decorative string around the filled box, then leaned over and gave her a peck on the cheek as he passed to deliver the cookies to the waiting customer.

Dani dropped to a chrome work stool and took a deep breath. There couldn't be another man in the world like Riley. Dani's Delights would never be the same without him. Neither would she, but she had known that going in.

ANGELA WAS FURIOUS. If Dani Boatman thought she was going to get away with treating her like that, she was dead wrong. Angela always found a way of getting back at people who mistreated her.

She shoved open the front door of the bakery. A man with a package in his hand blocked her path.

"That was quick," he said. "I didn't even ring the bell."

He scooted away from the door to allow a couple entrance to the shop. She started to shove him out of the way, but the company logo on the brown envelope caught her attention.

Corinthian Court Lab. This was the envelope James Haggard was looking for.

"Are you Dani Boatman?"

"Yes," she lied.

The man who was obviously new on this route handed her the electronic signature gadget. "Just sign here."

She signed Dani's name and took the package. She might give it to James. She might just toss it in the street. She walked to her car before opening the package. The enclosed document looked official.

"'Results of paternity testing,'" she read aloud.

She kept reading. She'd definitely call James. He'd owe her big-time for this.

THUNDER REVERBERATED THROUGH James Haggard's head as he read the lab report, growing louder and louder until he felt like a 747 was roaring through his skull.

The only woman he'd ever loved had been a slut. Not just in the later years when the addiction had turned her into a monster he didn't recognize, but in the beginning.

Amber slept in his bed, told him how much she loved him, made him feel like a king.

He'd done everything but kill for her, and he would have done that to keep her with him. And all the while she'd played him for a fool.

Lenny had told James from the first that he couldn't trust Amber, but it was his own brother he couldn't trust.

James read the last few lines of the test results and then threw the document to the floor of his beat-up pickup truck.

"I don't know why I'm shocked. Lenny treated me like I was stupid all my life. A stupid jerk who couldn't do anything right without him interfering, so why would he have any qualms about sleeping with my woman?"

"Who are you so angry with?" Angela asked. "Constance's mother or your brother?"

"Both, but Amber's no longer alive to taunt me. It's Lenny who's still cheating and double-crossing me."

"How?"

"He pushed and coerced me to go for the insurance settlement. Even when I wanted to drop it, he kept pushing."

Angela leaned over and picked up the forms. "I don't see how that's so bad. Why not go after the money? He must have thought you were the father."

"Lenny's a taker, not a giver. If there was any money to be gotten, it would have ended up in his pocket."

"I guess it will for sure now."

"No. It damn sure won't."

"How can you stop him? He's the father."

"He's also a wanted criminal who'd never be granted custody. That's why he pushed me to do it. That's why he kept harping about the birth certificate. He knew all along the DNA might show him as the father."

A plan began to coalesce in James's mind. "I'm going to need your help."

"Not if you're going to do something illegal."

"You left me passed out in my pickup truck on a deserted road the other night. You were lucky I didn't come back at you for that."

"That was Mother's doing. Remember? I told you. She goes ape when people get me high."

"You got yourself high. And you will help in whatever way I tell you to, or I'll leak those deep, dark secrets you told me. A dead child. The cover-up."

"Stop." She put her hands over her ears. "Stop saying those lies."

"If they were lies, they wouldn't be driving you

crazy. Now, here's what I want from you or your murderous secrets will climb out of their graves and drag you into the pits of hell with them."

AT LEAST HALF the tables in the bakery were taken and there were several people in line when the group of three nicely dressed young men walked in. They walked over to the counter but did not get in line.

"May I help you?" Dani asked.

"Actually, we're here to help you." One of the men flashed his FBI ID. Brad Grogan. "I'm looking for Riley Lawrence or Dani Boatman."

"I'm Dani. Give me a minute." She handed the bag of assorted muffins to her customer, then went and summoned her young assistant, Sandy, from the kitchen with instructions to take over for a few minutes.

"Could we talk somewhere private?" Brad asked.

"In my office, just off my kitchen. Riley is upstairs. I'll call him. He'll definitely want to hear what you have to say firsthand."

She called Riley while she led the men back to her office.

Riley bounded into the office a few minutes later. "Good news, I hope."

"Not for Lenny Haggard, but we're writing it up as a highly successful day for the FBI."

They introduced themselves and the one already identified as Brad took the lead.

"At twenty-two past twelve this afternoon, the

body of Lenny Haggard was found in one of the rental cabins at Bosley's Bait and Tackle. He died from three gunshots at close range to the back of his head."

"He's really dead?" Dani asked. "You're sure that was him?"

"No doubt about it."

"I can't believe I'm saying this about a murder, but that is the best news I've had in months, if not forever."

"His death will be a relief to a lot of innocent and not-so-innocent people," Brad agreed.

"That was quick," Riley said. "Less than twenty-four hours after we called with information that he was in Winding Creek, he's dead."

"It works that way more than you'd guess," Brad said. "We search for months, get a hot tip and then wham. We have our man."

"You said you found him dead. Does that mean it wasn't one of your guys who shot him?"

"That's what it means. Three shots to the back of the head is a trademark of Cecil Molina. Looks like one of his hatchet men got to Lenny before we could."

"That doesn't come as a real surprise, either," one of the other agents said. "He was so desperate to get his hands on your niece's trust fund he got careless. Stalking you. Showing his face around Winding Creek. Staying in a rental cabin that was registered in his brother's name. Careless errors. That's what desperation does."

"Do you have James Haggard in custody?" Riley asked.

"Not yet. We'll leave that to local law enforcement. Our agents have already talked to Sheriff Cavazos and he'll be talking to you about charging James with vandalism, harassment and an attempted scam to steal money."

"I doubt you'll see him again," the third agent said, "especially if he witnessed Lenny's murder. He'll be on the run and scared to death."

"Then this is over," Dani said. "My niece's biological father is dead, so he can make no claims on her trust fund. James Haggard isn't the father, but he is Constance's uncle."

"With an extensive criminal record, so his claim would never override yours. You can go back to running your shop."

"I'm ready to have that life back," she said.

"One more thing," Brad said. "We've been hearing about your cinnamon rolls and chocolate-filled croissants all day from the lucky team hanging out inside the bakery."

"So those were the guys consuming everything in sight. Can I offer you anything from my display case?"

"Thought you'd never ask."

"Take a seat and I'll serve you at your table.

My assistant will take your coffee order. It's all on the house."

Riley put his hand to the small of her back as they followed the team of agents into the serving area.

"What an ending to a wild ride," he whispered.

"It was that."

Only she wasn't ready for all the wildness to end.

"I'LL BE THERE for Tucker's goodbye dinner by six, I promise. I just have to take the ham-and-cheese croissants out of the oven and drop them off at the ladies auxiliary planning meeting," Dani said.

"We'll wait on you." Riley offered.

"No, we can't," Constance pleaded. "I won't get there in time to ride horses with Jaci if we don't leave now."

"Didn't you get enough of horses over the three days?" Dani asked.

"No. I have to practice a lot if I'm going to be a rodeo champion. We really need to live on a ranch."

"Better forget the ranch idea and stick with becoming a champion barrel racer. You have a far better chance of success with that." Dani gave Constance and Riley a quick hug and pushed them out the door.

It was early Friday evening. The streets were crowded with locals out for dinner, or shopping or just to grab an ice-cream cone or indulge in happy hour.

She wasn't afraid and she wasn't going to become

a prisoner in her own shop. Besides, Sheriff Cavazos had promised to have deputies in the area constantly until James Haggard was arrested or until they were sure he'd left town.

She walked into the kitchen and breathed in the quiet, safe familiarity of her surroundings. She would have Constance and her bakery for years to come. No place had ever felt more like home.

As for Riley, she couldn't imagine life without him, but she would never demand or even plead with him to stay in Winding Creek.

He was who he was. All she could do was love him for as long as he let her. And then she'd find a way to live with great memories and a breaking heart.

WHERE WERE HER car keys? Dani could swear she'd left them on the counter next to her croissants when she went back upstairs for her purse. Obviously she was mistaken, since they weren't there now.

She turned around and then realized they were in her pocket. Oh, well, it had been an exciting day.

Someone banged on the door. Hopefully it was FedEx since she was yet to receive the promised official copy of the lab report. She started toward the door and stopped when she saw Angela—no doubt here to complain about being fired.

Angela had problems and needed help, but Dani had a bakery to run. She didn't have the time, energy or expertise to take Angela on.

Still, she couldn't very well ignore her. She walked over and opened the door. "You caught me at a really bad time, Angela. I'm already running late for a dinner engagement."

"I'm not here to listen to your problems, bitch."

So this was how it was going to be. "Get out of my shop this minute before I call 911."

Angela shoved her hard, thrusting Dani back into the shop. "You want to keep living, you do as you're told."

Dani reached for her phone. Before she could punch in even one number, a large hand closed around her wrist and knocked the phone from her hands.

James Haggard had followed Angela in. The pistol clutched in his right hand was proof enough that this was not a visit to express his regrets.

"I didn't kill your brother," she said.

"I know. I did it. I killed the lying scum like I should have done years ago. Before he screwed me out of everything that mattered to me."

He took a step closer and pointed the gun at her head. "I'm through with being cheated. By Lenny, by Amber. By you."

"I've never cheated you, James. I don't have anything that belongs to you. Constance isn't your daughter. I have paternity testing that proves that." Unfortunately, she didn't have the copy at hand.

"I saw your tests."

"How could you?"

"It doesn't matter now. The results don't matter anymore. I've settled that score. You stole Constance's money and used it to buy this bakery. Money that belonged to me just as much as it belonged to you.

"No," he continued, anger hardening his voice. "I'm even more deserving. I took care of Amber when she was pregnant. You never came around."

He knew about the test results. She had no idea how he knew, but clearly discovering that Lenny was the father of Amber's child must have pushed him over the edge.

"The money was never yours or mine, and was never Lenny's, either," she said. "I would never steal from Constance. Never. The money is in a trust fund just like I said. I didn't lie to you. I'm not lying to you now."

"You're just like Lenny. All you do is run over people like me and Constance. I won't be run over again."

His face was twisted in rage. A cold, calculating rage. She'd never be able to talk sense into him. She needed a weapon or help from Angela. Only Angela had a blank look on her face, as if she was falling into a trance. No telling what she'd smoked, inhaled or shot into her veins.

There was no weapon in sight. Her only hope was to escape.

"I'm here to see that you finally get what you deserve, Dani Boatman."

"Please don't do this, James. If you kill me, you'll go to prison. Is that what you want?"

"Only the stupid ones go to prison. I'm not stupid. Get the knife and the tape, Angela. Bind her wrists and her ankles the way I instructed. There's no time to waste."

"Why are you with him, Angela? He's using you. You must see that."

"Shut up," Angela said, her voice suddenly shaky.

"Don't do it, Angela," Dani pleaded. "Don't let this monster ruin your life, too."

"She has no choice," James said. "No choice at all. She and her dirty little secrets belong to the devil and now to me."

Angela reached into her tote and pulled out a butcher knife and then two large rolls of duct tape, laying them all on one of the serving tables.

"Start with the wrists," James ordered.

"Don't do this," Dani pleaded. "If it's money you want, I'll find a way to get it for you."

"You had your chance. But you're just like Amber. You take and take and take. You never give."

"I'm nothing like Amber. I'll take good care of your niece. I love her with all my heart. Doesn't that matter to you?"

"The wrists. Now," James demanded. "I can't wait all night." He turned the gun toward Angela.

Dani's pulse raced. It was now or never.

She made a run for the kitchen. She tried to close the door behind her, but James was too fast. She careened onto the top of her solid worktable and slid the three feet across the surface on her stomach.

It took a few complicated moves to enable her to land on the floor feet first instead of head first.

She squatted down so that James couldn't see her, but now she could no longer see him. And there was nowhere else to run. If she went into her office, she'd be like a cornered rat.

She crawled on the floor behind the worktable, trying to find something she could use to defend herself. But there was nothing she could use to stop a bullet.

"Bring the tape," James bellowed. "Dani has to pay."

"I'm not going to prison for you. You're on your own," Angela shouted.

"You'll do as I say, you murdering bitch."

"Go to hell."

A shot sounded. The sound of Angela's scream reverberated sickeningly through the room.

"Why?" Dani screamed. "Why are you doing this?"

"Your slutty sister made a fool of me. So did Lenny. You're not going to get that chance. With you dead, all of Constance's money goes to me."

The bell over the front door rang and Dani heard noises drifting in from outside as the door opened and quickly closed again.

"What the hell?"

The voice was Riley's. Panic hit Dani hard and fast. She stood up behind the counter.

"It's James," she screamed. "In the kitchen. He has a gun."

James pointed the gun at her, his finger on the trigger. The evil that darkened his eyes said it all. He was going to kill her now.

Instinctively, she grabbed the two overflowing flour canisters by their rims and swung them one by one in rapid succession, the contents covering him as if it was a blizzard of snow.

James clawed at his face as the flour coated his fury-flamed eyes.

He shot at her, but the bullet flew wild. He turned at the sound of Riley's footsteps and fired in his direction. Fear paralyzed Dani as the shot rang out.

One shot, but it was James who went down.

A second later, Riley was on her side of the worktable and she was in his arms.

She held on tight as tears filled her eyes, washing streams of flour down her face. "Where's Constance?" she asked suddenly, realizing she wasn't there.

"Riding horses. We ran into Tucker at the feed store. I had this not-so-crazy premonition that we were not quite through with James. I sent her on with him and I put the pedal to the metal to get back to you."

"Quick Draw, to the rescue," she said, holding

him even tighter. She'd almost lost him. She never wanted to be that afraid again.

Seconds later sirens screamed. Riley held her tight until the bakery filled with paramedics and deputies.

James and Angela were both taken to the hospital.

Sheriff Cavazos arrived, took one look at the flour-strewn kitchen and shook his head. "You Lawrence brothers and your women bring a heck load of trouble to my county. Lucky for you that Dani sure can bake."

"Lucky for me," Riley said, "she sure can handle her flour."

Only she was the lucky one. She was alive and safe in Riley's arms.

# Epilogue

*One month later*

It was a beautiful Monday afternoon, a perfect day to enjoy the outdoors. But as much as Dani was enjoying her time with Grace while the girls were riding with Pierce, she was truly hoping to casually bump into Riley.

Up until a week ago, he'd been his usual self—attentive, sexy and always ready to make love or even to just hang out with her. For the past week he'd been mostly absent, claiming he was busy. When they were together, he seemed distracted.

She had a sinking feeling in her heart that he would soon be moving on. She'd promised herself she'd never ask for forever. Never ask him to give up the lifestyle he loved to become stuck in the town and the life she loved.

She never wanted him to feel trapped with her, but how was her heart going to survive without him?

Grace lifted her glass of lemonade and took a slow

sip. "Pierce is delighted Dudley Miles is being released from prison today. He credits you and Riley for most of that."

"It is a bizarre twist to a convoluted and incredible mystery," Dani agreed. Thankfully Angela survived the gunshot wound and decided to clear up much of the mystery."

"Still, I'm surprised Angela finally broke down and told the truth. I don't know her that well, but the few times I was around her, she showed no signs of grief or guilt."

"My guess is she just had the guilt and grief buried so deeply in her psyche she couldn't move past it. When James insisted she help him kill me, her psychological facade cracked."

"That's so sad and a very scary," Grace said.

"I'm just lucky and supremely grateful that never happened with Amber and Constance. Amber was my sister. Mother and I both loved her dearly and tried everything we could to keep help her kick the drugs. I wish now that I had tried even harder."

"You can't save everyone no matter how hard you try, but you have Constance now and she's a fantastic kid in spite of everything her mother put her through."

"You're right. I can't change the past anyway."

"How about a recap," Grace asked, "just to be sure I have all my facts straight?"

"I'll try. To start with, James is under arrest for attempted murder and for the murder of his brother,

Lenny. In the meantime he's receiving psychological assessments to determine if he's mentally stable enough to stand trial."

"And Angela?"

"She's admitted to being the only adult at home the day her son died. She got high and passed out. He climbed onto the counter, apparently trying to get a cookie. He fell and died from traumatic brain energy to the back of his head.

"She panicked, knowing she might face charges of neglect or manslaughter in his death. She tossed his body into the woods and then went home and told her family he'd been kidnapped from the house. The body was found months later and the evidence in the case soon pointed to Angela."

"But why would Dudley admit to the crime when he wasn't guilty?"

"To save Angela from going to prison. He and his wife, Millie, couldn't bear to see their precious, spoiled daughter take responsibility for anything. She's in a mental and psychological facility in Houston now, awaiting testing, treatment and eventually a trial."

"I read once that family ties can be the sweetest ones on earth or they can be as deadly as a blood-sucking leech," Grace said. "Sounds like the Miles family ties were definitely closer to the latter."

"Hopefully, they can make something good from all this."

"At least it's good that Dudley can go home. By

the way, what's up with Riley lately? He's always rushing off without saying where's he's going, and when he is here, he seems preoccupied."

"I haven't noticed," she lied, trying to keep the anxiety from her voice. She couldn't think about his leaving without getting literally ill.

Her cell phone dinged. She had a text from Riley.

Important that I see you and Constance. Can I take you two to dinner tonight at sixish?

He'd never asked her out by text before. More indication that this was the night the bomb would drop. No matter how upset she got, she wouldn't let him see her cry. There would be time enough for tears after he'd left.

RILEY SHOWED UP at ten after six and the three of them climbed into his pickup truck. Dani was a wreck, talking too much and too fast, nervously jumping from one subject to another.

It was a few minutes before she noticed he'd taken a back road that she was certain didn't lead to a restaurant. Still, she didn't ask questions. Maybe he just wanted a quiet place to talk and get this over with.

He turned in at a gate that said Wallace Ranch. They drove past acres and acres of fenced and cross-fenced pastures before stopping on a hill overlooking a small lake.

Constance bounded out of the backseat and then rushed off to chase a fluttering butterfly.

Riley opened the car door for Dani. They stood in silence for a few minutes, watching the sun set in the western sky.

"What do you think?" Riley asked.

"It's a beautiful area."

"I'm glad you think so. I put a down payment on this ranch today."

"You're buying this ranch?"

"It's not that incredible. I haven't bought anything before except pickup trucks, so I have the savings to be able to afford it."

"But what about your rambling ways and need to keep moving?"

"I think I was always just working my way to you. I want to marry you, Dani. I want to take care of you and Constance. I want to love you for the rest of my life."

Constance came running over and tugged on Riley's shirtsleeve. "Does this ranch have horses?"

"It will when we move out here. Horses and cattle and I'm thinking a big yellow dog."

"We're gonna have a ranch?" Constance asked.

"If your aunt whom I love very much will marry me?"

Constance started to jump up and down. "Say yes, Aunt Dani. Please say yes. Riley loves us and we love him. We'll be a family. With a ranch. And horses. And a dog!"

From heartbreak at the prospect of losing him to a marriage proposal. This was coming so fast. Her head was spinning. "What about my bakery?"

"We'll be like the elites, have a place in town and one in the country," Riley said. "Only difference is ours will be only fifteen minutes apart."

He took both her hands in his. "I would never expect you to give up the bakery any more than I'd give up ranching. I'll work the ranch during the day. You'll work at the bakery. Nights we'll be together at one place or the other. We can work it out."

It sounded like heaven, but...

"Are you sure this is what you want to do, Riley? "Are you very, very sure?"

He dropped to one knee, pulled a brilliant diamond solitaire from his pocket and slipped it onto her finger. "I'm very sure that there is no place in the whole world I'd rather be than with you. I love you more than I ever dreamed I could love anyone. Will you marry me, Dani Boatman, and make me the luckiest guy on the planet?"

"Yes. Yes. Yes." Tears filled her eyes. No one had the right to be this happy.

He stood and took her in his arms. Constance joined in the family hug and then dashed off to the nearest stump, jumped on top of it and started yelling to no one except perhaps the hidden wildlife this was moving to this ranch.

"What shall we do next?" Riley asked. "Eat. Go share our good news with the folks at the Double K?"

"Later," Dani whispered.

"Don't tell me this is one of those baking moments?"

"No, I just want to savor this feeling. But you never know what might come up once I get you in my bakery kitchen."

"No doubt. Ever since I met you I've been dreaming of escapades involving your whipped cream."

"I'll see that a lot of those dreams come true."

Riley Lawrence. No longer a rambling man but every inch a cowboy. The man she'd love every day for the rest of her life.

Who said you can't have it all?

\* \* \* \* \*

# INTRIGUE

## Available May 23, 2017

### #1713 HOT ZONE
*Ballistic Cowboys* • by Elle James
Army ranger Trace "Hawkeye" Walsh has no choice but to assist tough-as-nails rancher Olivia Dawson after he incapacitates her foreman, but his involvement on the ranch uncovers a dark conspiracy...and their own desires.

### #1714 CAVANAUGH STANDOFF
*Cavanaugh Justice* • by Marie Ferrarella
With a serial killer sweeping through Aurora, Detective Ronan Cavanaugh O'Bannon will do whatever it takes to protect one of Cavanaugh's own—even swallow his pride and work with wild-card detective Sierra Carlyle.

### #1715 THE WARRIOR'S WAY
*Apache Protectors: Tribal Thunder* • by Jenna Kernan
The entire city of Phoenix is under threat by ecoterrorists, and Turquoise Guardian and tribal police chief Jack Bear Den is working closely with loose cannon former FBI operative Sophie Rivas to save the day, even if it brings their dangerous attraction to the surface...

### #1716 MURDER IN BLACK CANYON
*The Ranger Brigade: Family Secrets* • by Cindi Myers
An FBI agent is murdered. A US senator goes missing. Loner PI Kayla Larimer will need to learn to trust Lieutenant Dylan Holt if she's going to make the connection between these crimes and the mysterious cult camped in the hostile Colorado wilderness.

### #1717 BODYGUARD WITH A BADGE
*The Lawmen: Bullets and Brawn* • by Elizabeth Heiter
Juliette Lawson is desperate to stay hidden from her dangerous cop ex-husband—desperate enough to take FBI sniper Andre Diaz hostage in order to escape Quantico—but when Andre learns the truth of her past, he knows he's the man to keep her safe.

### #1718 SON OF THE SHEIK
*Desert Justice* • by Ryshia Kennie
After a one-night stand with playboy and investigator Talib Al-Nassar left her pregnant, Sara Elliott fled Morocco, but when she returns to teach her son about his roots her secret is discovered—and the only man with the power to protect her son is his father.

---

**YOU CAN FIND MORE INFORMATION ON UPCOMING HARLEQUIN® TITLES, FREE EXCERPTS AND MORE AT WWW.HARLEQUIN.COM.**

SPECIAL EXCERPT FROM

# ⬢ HARLEQUIN®

# I N T R I G U E

*Detective Ronan Cavanaugh O'Bannon will do
whatever it takes to protect one of the Cavanaughs' own
from a serial killer sweeping through Aurora, including
working with wild-card detective Sierra Carlyle.*

*Read on for a sneak preview of
CAVANAUGH STANDOFF,
the next book in USA TODAY bestselling author
Marie Ferrarella's fan-favorite series
CAVANAUGH JUSTICE.*

He knew he had to utilize her somehow, and maybe she could be useful. "All right, you might as well come along. You might come in handy if there's a next of kin to notify." Ronan began walking back to his car. "I'm not much good at that."

"I'm surprised," Sierra commented.

Reaching the car, Ronan turned to look at her. "If you're going to be sarcastic—"

"No, I'm serious," she told him, then went on to explain her rationale. "You're so detached, I just assumed it wouldn't bother you to tell a person that someone they'd expected to come home was never going to do that again. It would bother them, of course," she couldn't help adding, "but not you."

Ronan got into his vehicle, buckled up and pulled out in what seemed like one fluid motion, all the while chewing on what this latest addition to his team had just said. Part of him just wanted to let it go. But he couldn't.

"I'm not heartless," he informed her. "I just don't allow emotions to get in the way and I don't believe in using more words than are absolutely necessary," he added pointedly since he knew that seemed to bother her.

"Well, lucky for you, I do," she told him with what amounted to the beginnings of a smile. "I guess that's what'll make us such good partners."

He looked at her, stunned. He viewed them as being like oil and water—never able to mix. "Is that your take on this?" he asked incredulously.

"Yes," she answered cheerfully.

The fact that she appeared to have what one of his brothers would label a "killer smile" notwithstanding, Ronan just shook his head. "Unbelievable."

"Oh, you'll get to believe it soon enough," she told him. Before he could say anything, Sierra just continued talking to him and got down to the immediate business at hand. "I'm going to need to see your files on the other murders once we're back in the squad room so I can be brought up to date."

He didn't even spare her a look. "Fine."

"Are you always this cheerful?" she asked. "Or is there something in particular that's bothering you?"

*Don't miss*
*CAVANAUGH STANDOFF by Marie Ferrarella,*
*available June 2017 wherever*
*Harlequin® Intrigue books and ebooks are sold.*

www.Harlequin.com

HIEXP0517

# JUST CAN'T GET ENOUGH?

Join our social communities
and talk to us online.

You will have access to the latest
news on upcoming titles and special
promotions, but most importantly,
you can talk to other fans about your
favorite Harlequin reads.

Harlequin.com/Community

Facebook.com/HarlequinBooks

Twitter.com/HarlequinBooks

Pinterest.com/HarlequinBooks

# THE WORLD IS BETTER WITH

## Romance

Harlequin has everything from contemporary, passionate and heartwarming to suspenseful and inspirational stories.

Whatever your mood, we have a romance just for you!

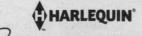

# Love the Harlequin book you just read?

### Your opinion matters.

Review this book on your favorite book site, review site, blog or your own social media properties and share your opinion with other readers!

**Be sure to connect with us at:**
Harlequin.com/Newsletters
Facebook.com/HarlequinBooks
Twitter.com/HarlequinBooks